Luv Me

Also by Wanda D. Hudson

Wait for Love

Dating Wanda

 *Miss Luv's Books*

®*Miss Luv's Books*

Because Everybody Needs A Little Luv!

Miss Luv's Books

www.wandadhudson.com

Copyright © 2008 by Wanda D. Hudson

First Printing 2008

ISBN 13: 978-0-9815325-0-9

ISBN 10: 0-9815325-1-9

LCCN: 2008900922

Printed In The United States of America

Cover Design: CANDACEK –www.cckwebdev.com

Formatting: Final Touch Media Solutions

ACKNOWLEDGEMENTS

Doobah, thank you for being Mommy's Doobah. I luv you.

Diana, I told you everybody wants your Mama! I luv you.

T. Rhythm Knight, thank you for your literary expertise. I would not have published these stories without your excellent and honest critique.

Shaye "Butta" Gray. Once again you smoothed it out. Your vision, your comments – AMAZING. Thank you. Imitation spreads come and go, but there is nothing as sweet as Butta!

Linda Wilson, I thank you! You're good girl – keep on doing what you do.

Thank you to everyone who supported my first novel, Wait for Love: A Black Girl's Story. Please continue to ride with me. The WandaLuv literary journey will be more than satisfying.

And now, just like the aforementioned, it is your turn to LuvMe.

Wanda D. Hudson

Dear Diary

June 18, 2007

I've always wanted one of those dark chocolate men. The kind of darkness that makes you wonder if the skin hurts. The hue almost has a purple bluish tint, but it eludes this shade. Some women like the high colored man, yellow, a red bone that is close enough to white as a black person can get. Something about the dark is sexy to me. Doing it in the dark is stimulating, warm, and cozy. Even with the lights off the world can see a light man do his thing. But a dark man – umph, mysterious deep heat surrounds him. I want to get sexually tingled by his warmth.

Although his luv to me is still a mystery, his appearance is something that I know very well. He's sexy. That's all my eyes can see about him. A sexy man that I want to explore. I don't want to talk. I want to lick him, to smell him, to squeeze him into my heart and make him luvme.

Staring at someone each time you see them and not saying a word so simple like, hello, is called visual stalking. A court date was calling my name each time I saw him. Moisture always evades my throat making my voice hard, which gave it the right to disobey my non-existent command to open. One day I plan to take him – to tear his clothing from his body and own all that he was born with.

The bow of his legs, the spread of his back, ooh, his deep brown ass has to be my glory. Last week I saw him in a form-fitting tee shirt. Women rave over a six-pack. His is a quarter of a keg. A six-pack fills you up, but a keg puts you out. A man's keg tears you down and makes you beg for forgiveness in tongues. That's what I want. I want for him to finish with me – just use me, and make me walk like a three-legged dog, or hop like a one-legged frog. I want to whimper and still await his return.

What I have is more than a simple crush. It's a luv sickness that consumes me. My stomach flips, my eyes flutter, and I have nearly fainted when he passes. He changes his cologne often and each time the scent pulls me closer to him. He is the leader of my mind. My nostrils inhale him deeper and deeper until a passionate confusion kisses me. This dark man was meant to luvme.

My body is not that of a perfect ten. No woman's is. Everyone has something that does "it" for them. I have breasts that will fit his hands. Ass that he can palm, lips that he will kiss, and legs that he will wrap around his neck and back, and hold onto as he sucks me into his darkness.

He has a woman. My jealously is hard to contain. I smile occasionally at her when I see her. The truth is I hate her. She does "it" for him. He never looks my way. I've tried a few things to get him to notice me. If I'm allowed the chance to walk in front of him I switch my ass up a notch. My skirts have gotten shorter, and the lip colors that I wear I imagine he knows will coat his shaft nicely. Yellow and blue make green, red and blue make purple, and my color of bronze brown and his black make luv.

I want what they have together. Realizing that if I had him he wouldn't luvme the same as he luvs her is what keeps me away. What they share is special. She is lucky and she knows it. Sometimes she flaunts it. Hell, I would parade that beautiful back man, too.

Right now I can see his lips taking her nipple into his mouth…umph, all I can do is imagine that it is I who was in her place. He pleases her, she pleases him, and they are satisfied together. Doing it in color is delicious - doing it in his dark is sweet heaven.

For now I have to obey the rules of their relationship. I know she has laid down the law with him. She has told him that he belongs to her. I would tell him that if he were mine. He will never look my way. He will never look at any woman and desire her as long as she has him.

Still I wonder -- if I were she, would he luvme?

LuvMe

H-Ball Queen
A New Haven
DSL
Work the Stick in My Ride
This Rhythm Is Rated L
T-Xtasy Talk
Reaching A Peak
Room With A View
LuvMe Quick - SHE
C-Wrap
Soul Reverie
So Succulent
One Night Stand…Or Two
LuvMe Quick – 42nd Street
New Year's Eva

H-Ball Queen

Eva stumbled her way through the crowd seconds before the store was to close. Her best friend, Sheila, told her to go to a bootleg version of a Spencer's Gift store in hopes of finding the perfect Halloween outfit. After two patrons stepped on her toes, Eva practiced cursing Sheila out.

"Why do I continue listening to her ass?"

The only thing more aggravating than the disorderly shoppers was the fact that Eva didn't change out of her three-inch, block-heeled, open-toed shoes after work. Thinking that the time it would take to give her feet comfort would slow her down was a mistake.

The sound over the PA stating that the store would close in less than ten minutes gave her an adrenalin rush. She always waited until she had no other choice to do any kind of holiday shopping, and Halloween was no different. Of course Sheila had talked her into attending some kind of adult masquerade thingy called The H-Ball. Eva outwardly denied that she didn't want to go but desperately desired a change of pace. She was single and thought the party would provide her with a mate who wanted the same type of love she desired.

The greasy haired, bucked-tooth, overworked cashier who looked as if he lived in his parent's basement, and jacked off to porn daily called out, "Next," in a tired voice.

"I'll take this."

The warm smile on her face quickly changed to a deep blush when the store was alerted to her pending purchase.

"Price check at register three on a Purple Riding Hood cape and thong set. It also has a half mask and a purple whip."

The sales clerk turned to Eva and smirked, knowing he'd outright embarrassed her. Her mild humiliation continued for a few more seconds, as the price blasted throughout the store.

"Fifty-three ninety-nine for the purple thong set. Ya hear me, Harold?"

Keying the numbers in with his grubby hands, Harold said, "Yeah," and looked at Eva as if she were a freak waiting for him to unleash her.

She continued to face the cashier. Her back burned, no doubt from the glaring looks from the other shoppers, but hey, they were in the store doing the same thing she was. Vigorously, she pulled out her Visa card and slid it towards the worker.

"Here, this should take care of it," and then Eva looked over her shoulder and gave a sassy nod to let other's know she wasn't humiliated.

As the cashier continued the transaction, her cell phone rang.

"Hello?"

"Hey, what's up? Did you find a costume yet?"

It was Sheila calling to make sure she hadn't changed her mind about the evening's festivities.

"Yes. I'm leaving the store now. What time are you picking me up?"

"Marisol and I will be there at ten. What are you wearing?"

Irritation filled her as she said, "Marisol?" You didn't tell me that sleaze was going, too?"

"Are you two still at odds over the bet? Eva, let it go. Besides, she has free tickets."

"Tsk. A bet is a bet. She owes me fifty dollars. Her dumb ass shouldn't have opened up her mouth if she didn't have the money."

In a soothing voice Sheila continued, "Baby, you know how Marisol is. All talk. You need to relax and not let her get to you. Now, about tonight. What are you wearing?"

Answering as she fumbled to find the keys to her car, "A Purple Riding Hood thong and cape set."

"Oh, that sounds nasty. I'm going as a dominatrix Mother Hubbard. I want some dick all up in my cubbard, cupboard, shelves…you name it."

Eva stopped in her tracks and doubled over with laughter. No matter what her mood was, Sheila always came through with something to put a smile on her face.

"Hurry up and get home and changed. We are going to get buck tonight, girl."

"I don't know about all of that, but I'll live a little."

"That's a deal. See'ya at ten."

After making a stop at a chicken joint to grab a bite to eat, Eva headed home to a warm bath and mood music.

"Let's see, Brian and Gerald, the two of them - ooh, if only."

Once she had her costume on she pranced around her place like a tiger stalking its prey. If this party didn't raise her up out of her man funk, she didn't know what would.

At ten p.m. sharp, Eva heard Marisol's car horn.

"That shit even beeps in her native tongue."

Eva's dislike of Marisol went deeper than their bet over who would get the most numbers at a club one night. Marisol was a sexy, brown-skinned Dominican, with long, wavy black hair, and deep-set tempting eyes. Her figure was an icy eight, her skin held no blemishes, and every man they came in contact with approached Marisol first.

Eva took a deep breath to calm herself before leaving her place. She threw on her swing coat, promptly turned off the music and the lights, and strutted to the vehicle. Sheila swung the back door open and held out her hand along with a bottle of E&J Brandy.

"Come on in, girl! Join the party!"

It was obvious that Sheila was drunk. Marisol didn't drink and if the three of them hung out together she was usually the designated driver. Eva rolled her eyes at the sound of the radio blasting as their entire bodies swerved to the groove. She frowned her face as she situated herself in the car. "E&J? I'm not drinking that awful stuff. That's rock gut liquor."

"Look, don't start that Miss Prissy shit tonight! You betta take it to the head!"

Giving a hand signal and rolling her eyes, Eva responded, "Hell no."

Sheila took a swig, and then returned the bottle to Eva's face.

"When was the last time you had some dick?"

Marisol's eyes met Eva's straight on. She wanted to hear if her nemesis was as lonely as she was, and turned to see her face as she told her secret.

"Hand me the bottle."

Not one to easily bow to the victor, Eva turned the bottle to her lips and grimaced as the warm concoction burned her throat. After suppressing a cough and maintaining a tough look, she took another swig and settled into the seat comfortably.

"Drive this bitch," came from Sheila in a commanding voice. Marisol obeyed and cranked up the system a little louder as she drove her cohorts to their destination.

They were halfway down the road from the party spot and could hear the music blasting. Eva had drunk one fourth of the pint of E&J and was ready for whatever the night had in store.

"Oh, shit...that's my jam." Eva began to sing in a half slur. "I dance when I pull my pants and do the rock-a-wear, now lean back...lean back...lean back...lean..."

Laughing, Sheila said, "What are you saying?"

"Leave me alone, girl. Lean back...lean back..."

Sheila and Marisol giggled as the valet approached.

"I'll take it from here, lovely ladies. You can hop in the van and ride to the door, or walk. It's up to you."

"I think we'll walk. We need some air," was Marisol's reply."

The three of them walked in a sexy spell as Eva continued to hum off key. When they were about two feet from the door, Shelia stopped them and made an announcement.

"Ah, I have something to tell you, Eva. Ah, this isn't just a masquerade party. It's an orgy ball."

A few seconds of silence passed before Eva spoke, quite flustered.

"An orgy! Did you say orgy? What the fuck! You should have told me this sooner! Take me home!"

"Just calm down. Listen, you don't have to participate in anything, and if you decide to do something, you have on a mask. Loosen up."

Through her ho bunny costume mask, Marisol stared at Eva hard in her face. She sneered with glee at her fright.

"Dime si te asusta un poco de sexo?"

Eva lived in a predominantly Spanish-speaking neighborhood and picked up bits of the language that way. She knew enough to understand what Marisol said.

"Don't start that shit with me, Marisol! Skank, I'm not scared of nothing. Move out of my way!"

"Ah, apuesto a todos los hombres se congregan a mí. Usted puede saber mis sobras."

Sheila gave Marisol a light nudge.

"Knock it off. Don't agitate her anymore."

Eva stepped towards Marisol and stood directly in her face.

"I can handle this. Look, bitch. I know you said something about men and sex, but I will have a good time tonight. And no, I don't want your leftovers."

"Usted puede venir a mi casa y mirar tan usted no estará solitario."

"Whatever. Move out of my way. I have a party to start."

Sheila and Marisol each stepped to the side and watched Eva stroll to the door quite fierce. She left her coat in the car and her purple cape swayed with each step of her four-inch stilettos, which made her long caramel-colored legs calve muscles flex. Her straight-pressed hair swayed from side to side, while her firm, tight booty pouted and bumped. Feeling and looking sexy pumped her up. When she reached the door she turned and said, "Well, what are you tricks waiting on? Come on."

Although there was animosity between Eva and Marisol, the three of them entered through the doors arm in arm. They stood in a massive entryway that had four different doorways in it. The ceilings were high with a skyscraper effect, and held decorations of many kinds. There were ghouls and goblins adorned with sexy lingerie or nothing at all. The faces were a bit spooky, but you quickly forgot about that when you saw the body. Large, long various colored muscles of pleasure draped the males, and the female ones had a variety of decorated meowing cats. Some were shaved, or hairy, and had tattoos of sexual positions on them.

The scent of sweet sexual musk filled the air and journeyed their mind away from the day's activities. With each inhale of it, Eva imagined she was with the man that would make her forget everything that troubled her. There were a few pieces of furniture placed about with people engaged in foreplay or full-blown fucking. Eva drew her forefinger to her lips and sucked it lusciously for a few moments. Just as she opened her mouth to speak, a man wearing only a mask with a condom attached to the side of it approached them.

"Hi, I'm Adam from the Garden of Eden. How are you ladies this evening?"

Eva's eyes traveled Adam's tall, mystic, mocha frame swiftly. They rested on his smooth, brown, slightly curved partner that looked to be about seven inches. It wasn't hard, but it hung deliciously, awaiting a nice, comfy, warm spot to rest in.

"We're fine, Adam."

Sheila spoke, being she was the only one not flabbergasted by a man's penis.

Adam continued his greeting. "Let me give you a brief rundown of the party. As you can see, there are four doors ahead of you. Door one leads to Desire Destiny. When you walk through those doors, all you have to do is ask for what you want and you shall receive it. Door two will take you to Lesbian Lust. I don't think I have to explain that any further. Door three is Strictly Dickly. It's for men and women, so if there are certain things you don't want to see, don't go in there."

Sheila elbowed Eva when she noticed she was still staring at Adam. Marisol's eyes roamed the room and landed on a fountain with a thick white substance flowing from it. Employing a voice that men always fell victim to, she asked, "Adam, please tell me what scrumptious treat that fountain holds?"

"That would be what we call the Enchantment Cascade. Some people like to use it as lubrication, take baths in it, or just drink it."

"Daaayum…" Sheila said this in anticipation of tasting a bit herself.

Adam stroked himself before he responded, "Ladies, whatever your wildest dreams are, you can have them fulfilled at the H-Ball."

"Oooh, and what's behind door number four?"

Eva was beginning to salivate and began to mist just thinking of what would happen to her that evening.

"Ladies, door number four leads you to the H-Ball. It's a contest. Instead of bobbing for apples, you get on your knees and show the world what kind of ball slobbing skills you have. The person that makes their partner cum first, be it male on male, or female to male, wins three thousand dollars. Any of you ladies down?"

Eva needed a nice down payment for the new car that she had her mind set on, but sucking a stranger's balls? She squirmed at the feel of her wet thong and positioned her mask firmly as she thought about the money she could possibly win.

A waitress approached with a tray of liquid goodies. Without hesitation or asking, Eva reached for a short round glass. She held the glass on her lips for a moment to quickly sniff the contents. Satisfied, she downed the smooth, heated Hypnotic liquid. Her mouth still held the flavor as she asked Adam to be her partner at the H–Ball.

"I'm down, Adam. Are you?"

"Wait a minute, I'm sure Adam would like the woman of his choice. Who do you have in mind? Haga no usted desea a una mujer atractiva como yo mismo?" Marisol stepped forward a bit and awaited his response to her.

Reaching his arms out he said, "I thought you'd never ask. Let's go. We have to sign up. The contest begins at midnight."

Adam took Eva's hand in his and they strode away with Sheila looking on in delight, and Marisol very frustrated.

"Marisol, just be happy for her, okay? There are plenty of men to go around."

Satisfied, they watched them walk thru the doors as Eva turned and mouthed, "I'll see you beeyatches later."

The door closed with Adam and Eva on the inside. Secretly, Marisol had always wanted to be with a woman, so she headed for Lesbian Lust.

Sheila wanted four men, two on the top and two on the bottom. Just the thought of having her nipples caressed, along with a back massage, enthralled her. That, added with a nice slow clit sucking and anal teasing, would satisfy her for a few days. She waved goodbye to Marisol and headed into Desire Destiny.

Inside the H-Ball room, Adam and Eva walked hand in hand. He had no qualms about his nudity and his openness aided Eva. She had a few more shots of Hypnotic and felt like she could dribble his balls painlessly and with style. During the time leading up to the contest, the two of them bumped and grinded around the room, with Adam teasing and tempting her various holes. He turned and twisted Eva's body in ways she'd never experienced. He raised her leg over his shoulder as they stood and ran his hand up and down her thigh.

Feeling bolder than she'd ever felt, Eva asked, "Adam, after the contest can we go to Desire Destiny?"

"Yes. Do you want only me, or do you want someone else?"

"You have me going right now. I want you."

"Good. That's what I wanted to hear. Turn around."

Eva lowered her leg and did as Adam instructed. With her back towards him, he bent her forward and circled around her ass and hole.

"Girl, you have a serious onion back here. Are you going to make me cry?"

"If you slice it right you won't have any tears."

"Oh, this is going to be a good night."

She turned to face him and their eyes signaled their passion to begin. Intertwining tongues pulled their bodies close, and Eva wrapped her legs around his body as he lifted her into the air. In the past she had always fallen easily for men and she had to keep in mind where she was, and in what context. Just as she felt herself slipping, a booming voice came out over the speakers in place of the music.

"Ladies and Gentlemen, it's time for the H-Ball to begin. Take your places."

"Are you ready, sexy?"

"For easy money? Lead the way."

Adam led Eva to their place in the line. They were the seventeenth couple to sign up, so respectively, they stood in the seventeenth spot. There were thirty-five couples in all, and at this point, she felt she was a shoo-in to win. The liquor in her system wouldn't let her lose, and feeling anything on a man amped her up even more.

All of the couples stood face to face, and then the music began. Lean Back blared in the room and Eva became a stripper in search of a pole. She flung her cape off and worked her bra and thong covered caramel body to the floor in a seductive rhythm. Adam did his thing by standing erect and spreading his legs. He leaned back, as the song drilled, which made him protrude out further. Adam's pelvis thrust forward in hopes of hitting the bottom of Eva, but the thought of what he'd do to her later kept him going strong.

Eva was now on the floor and directly between Adam's legs. She turned her body over to get a better grip on his balls. Her palms were on the floor and she spread her thighs wide. Gently placing Adam's meaty sacs in her mouth and rolling and gyrating her hips, she slowly began to suck delicately. Through the music she could hear Adam calling her name soft and sweet.

"Oh, Eva. Make that money, girl. Eva's gonna get paid. Eva. Eva. Eva."

Momentarily, Eva turned her head to the left and right to check out her competition. The couple on her right was arguing, but Eva couldn't figure out what they were saying. One of the moderators of the contest approached them and they were disqualified on the spot. The girl on her left was working her mouth like an old pro. Eva stole a few of her moves and Adam dipped his body down a bit to show his enjoyment.

"Damn, I'm going to marry you."

Eva smiled at Adam's comment as she continued slobbing to get a release from him. One of the rules was that you couldn't stroke or fondle the balls with your hands. Just like bobbing for apples, it was all mouth action.

"We have a winner," was announced and the room was filled with groans.

"Hold on, peeps. We have to inspect it."

Eva dropped down to her knees and lowered her head. Her jaws were beginning to tense up but she had enjoyed feeling Adam in her mouth. Adam leaned forward and kissed her on the top of her head.

"Don't worry about it, sexy. We have the rest of the night together."

Adam was about to help Eva stand up when another announcement filled the room.

"That was a false alarm people. Pre-cum doesn't count."

The music started again. Getting into a good groove, Eva positioned her body once again under Adam. As she moved closer to Adams balls, she saw dollar signs on them, and planned to roll in that money later that night.

Using more tongue, and lifting her body back and up to rotate her tongue inside his thighs made Adam shout out in ecstasy.

"Ahhhh, yes, it's on now! Ahhhh, yes, girl! Yes!"

Sliding back down and firmly grasping his balls with her lips did the trick. Eva filled her mouth with saliva and bobbed her mouth up and down on Adam's balls as if she were dunking them in an all-natural cleansing solution. Her jaws tensed up as she held them in her mouth and squeezed, releasing their contents thru his erect dick.

"Oh shit! Ahhhh!" Adam screamed like it was his first time.

Hot semen spewed out across the room as she sat up panting, waiting to hear the official word.

"Ladies and Gentlemen, we have a winner. The H-Ball is over. Enjoy the rest of your night."

Adam helped her to her feet and they followed two moderators to a back room to collect her cash prize. Adam walked closely behind with everything he had aimed at her ass. When she bent slightly to pick the moneybag up off the table, he quickly slid his condom on, spread her cheeks slightly, and slid into her from behind.

"Oh, ah, oh…" were the only words Eva could muster.

"I think we better leave them alone," came from one of the moderators.

The other people in the room left without closing the door behind them. Adam placed his hands around Eva's hips and gently pulsated in and out of her. She bent over further to receive all of him as she pulled her money close to her flailing breasts.

"Do it, Adam. Do it to me good." Eva rotated her hips and pushed her ass out further, enabling him to go deeper. He bent forward and ran his tongue up and down her back and pounded her harder.

Eva trembled as she squirted juice down her legs and on the floor. Adam once again released his goods as they both relaxed momentarily before he spoke.

"Damn, baby. All that was for me?"

"Are you worth it?"

"Hell, yeah. I have never cum from just ball sucking. You got skills. I have a confession, though. I didn't care if you won or not, I just entered the contest to get treated. Do you forgive me?"

"I have three thousand dollars in my hands. Do you think I forgive you?" Adam and Eva burst out laughing and hugged.

"How about a nice shower before heading into Desire Destiny?"

"You have a deal. They walked out of the room hugged up like lovers and Adam asked, "So, Eva, will you be my date next year?"

Confidently she replied, "Of course. This event was created with me in mind. I'm the reigning H-Ball Queen. I must return to defend my title."

A New Haven

I never noticed Jackson until I saw him without any obstructions. He had sat behind me in our Customer Service training class for almost a week, and in my small corner of the universe, he didn't exist. That is until he removed his spectacles. He became the object that made my heart pound when I saw him.

It was as if he had a Superman effect. Nerdy precise movements with a tad bit of genius surrounded him when he took in everything with four eyes. When he removed his glasses, he changed to a dark prince who had the smoothness of rich fine gold. One morning I turned around to look at the clock on the wall that hung a few feet above his head, and I saw what was hiding in plain sight. Oh, was he fine. I fought with a perplexed look on my face to turn away but I couldn't. My mind questioned me. Is that the same man? Look again…look again.

A few minutes later I dropped my ink pen on the floor and bent to pick it up slowly. Quickly, I cut my eyes in his direction. He had on his glasses, which made me frown. Silently, I began to wonder if I was tired and only imagined that I'd seen an irresistible man.

For over a year I had been single and was coming up on the dreaded anniversary of my hurtful breakup. I hadn't ventured into the arena of a man since and missed the male companionship. It could have simply been that my wants had overpowered my needs, which made me see Jackson as the man that could complete my missing jigsaw puzzle piece.

In two days, four hours and sixteen minutes my anniversary would arrive. Malloy and I had been dating for three years. We had spoke of marriage and were on our way to pick out an engagement ring. I told him that I didn't like the fact that after all this time we were still only considered girlfriend and boyfriend. I felt that being someone's girlfriend was a title you held proudly in High School, not one that befit a thirty-three-year-old woman. I wanted a commitment from him or I would end things. He said he loved me, which I felt he did as much as he could. If we ever arrived at the jewelers, he most likely would have picked the cheapest ring to get me to shut up.

We had a pleasant conversation for the bulk of our ride, and then the inside of the car went into a tailspin that up until recently I hadn't been able to straighten out. Malloy point blank told me that he had been involved with another woman and would continue to see her after purchasing my ring. He boasted that he wasn't ready to stop seeing her and our relationship may have been different if I hadn't pressured him into marrying me. The stabbing feeling came when he added that he couldn't marry a woman who was simply "okay" in bed, and that was the reason he had begun a new relationship. Basically, there was nothing for me to say.

Malloy had been my haven, my security net. I never thought that he wouldn't be around to lookout for me. He pulled the car over and let me out at a bus stop, the only shelter I could find afterward. Previously I rode the bus on the same dismal day every month, but now I plan only do it after a year has passed. Today my luck may change. This may be the day I was born to live for. If Jackson reciprocates my emotions, my bus pass will be taken away.

The instructor gave the class a ten-minute break and I went to the ladies room. Splashing cold water on my face took my temperature down and stopped the imminent sweat beads that were threatening to crack my concealer. I hadn't felt the so-called vapors for a man in such a long time that I didn't quite know how to handle myself. Although I probably wouldn't approach him I wished I had sat next to him. If I could have seen him through his, I have no personality style glasses, I would have. Now I have two challenges in front of me. One, retain the knowledge that is presented to me and two, obtain a man in the process.

When I exited the ladies room Jackson was standing directly across the hall in front of the door. His rear side faced me and I saw his strong muscular back through his long-sleeved light blue dress shirt. His gluteus protruded and showed off maximum firmness. I ran my tongue over my lips outwardly showing my desire to hold every inch of his body. Then he turned around. His glasses caused my mouth to drop open slightly and gave me a look of stupidity. I quickly regrouped and walked back into the classroom without as much as offering a smile in his direction.

It was as if he was playing a game with me. He reeled me in only so far and then cast me out to a distance suitable of bobbing for survival. Once again I had to see if he was indeed the same man of my mystery. The instructor hadn't returned back to the class yet so I turned around again, pretending that I had to ask a question of the woman that sat two seats over from him. She wasn't in her seat, which I knew before I made my rotation, so I played it off by making small chatter with Jackson. He had removed his glasses once again and was cleaning them off. Secretly, I hoped he dropped them on the floor and in my haste to pick them up I'd mistakenly step on them.

"How do you like the class?"

I should have said something clever, but the sight of him conquered my vocabulary.

He cleared his voice gently before he spoke.

"It's very informative."

After his last answer in a deep baritone voice, he rolled his eyes in exasperation. It had a comical feel to it and made us both laugh. The last instructor we were for forced to listen to made staring at lint balls seem lively.

I had him bare at that point. I'd do anything to keep him that way.

"So, what shift do you work? I can't say that I've ever seen you in the facility before."

His eyes examined mine as he spoke.

"Oh, you've seen me. I work the same shift as you, but on the other side of the plant. We usually pass each other in the parking lot, or in the cafeteria."

Instantly my facial expression distorted as I tried to figure out the first or the last time that I saw him. He eased my confusion by answering my question before it was posed to him.

"I've been on vacation for the last week, but I saw you in payroll before that. I was a few people behind you when we had to come in and sign for our checks the week the computers went haywire."

He spoke in a seductively slow motion that made the dormant butterflies in my body flutter with excitement.

Excitedly I responded.

"Oh, yes, I remember! My name is Sherita Styles. And you are?"

I slid my hand out knowing he'd respond. I had to feel him. I had to have a chance to hold onto him and caress him with the ease I was sure he had been missing.

"Jackson Harris. It's nice to meet you, Sherita. That's such a pretty name and it fits you perfectly."

We held hands as a quiet moment consumed us. The rest of the class was full of busy conversations, but once we touched, the noise that surrounded us was blocked out. I took his face in and saw every feature that had been subdued by his black square frames. His eyes extended a one-way entrance down a smooth spicy dark chocolate road. I devoured it as I traveled to my destination. He had sucked me in and I wouldn't allow him to let me go. His skin was sinfully alluring and held a haunting mystical glow about it. I followed it down to his neck, where my visual show was abruptly cut short by his shirt collar. My sight returned to the upward path and landed on his mouth. Jackson' plump lips were adorned by a groomed mustache and goatee with a hint of gray. Sexy. His face felt like the safe haven that I had longed for. Joining with him would be the same as going home to a familiar comfort zone.

He was a gorgeous creature without his glasses. Love at first sight had been unheard of prior to meeting him. All of that changed when we touched. Instantly he became my man. His hands were calming and soothing. I closed my eyes and felt them sliding around my body. With ease I could see us in our bedroom with him taking charge of my passions. He was the man that I could submit to without any commands.

"Sherita, are you alright?"

A low moan escaped me in my silent moment of wonderment. There I sat in front of him with my eyes closed and vulnerable to him in a room full of people. I felt like a fool.

Promptly I opened my eyes.

"Oh, excuse me. I was thinking of something else I had to do this evening. Sorry." I released his hand and returned to my forward facing position.

Throughout the remainder of the day I stole glances at him. He saw me staring at him a few times, but I didn't care that I had been busted. My heart was his without any constraints.

When the class was dismissed I walked to my car in a heavenly lull. My imagination saw Jackson and me walking together and him opening my door. When we were both strapped in we would ride home discussing the days events. Once there we would have a candlelight dinner that would evolve into a daily event. Then, we would bathe together and treat each other to our splendid bodies before drifting off to sleep.

The sound of a door closing pulled me out of my beloved daze. Jackson had parked his car next to mine and before today I probably wouldn't have noticed. I turned to see him sitting upright and getting ready to pull off. He had his glasses on again but I made myself wave and smile. I could see my body and contact lens in his future. From this day forward I'd do anything I could to make him see that I was the woman for him.

Most of my evening was spent thinking about Jackson. I had moved into my apartment after Malloy and I parted and usually didn't do much of anything when I was home. This night I fantasized about the man with the alter ego. I swear with those glasses he looked like a newsroom guppy. A fish that was eager to read press releases and run to the editor every time a story broke. In his frames he was the geek who typed all of the copy and made sure there were no mistakes present.

When his glasses were removed he looked like the news anchor that was too suave for words. He could be an actor, every woman's prince, and a calendar or Playgirl centerfold pullout. I wanted to hang him on my wall, in front of my mirror and just take in his debonair delight for all it had to offer.

The next morning I awoke two hours before my alarm clock spoke. I decided to take a bubble bath and soak in my thoughts of Jackson. We had one more week of classes and with him in such close proximity of me I wanted to make sure he noticed me. I bathed in honeysuckle milk foam. Someone told that on my body it omitted a scent that was the same as the queen bee that dominated her hive. After hearing that, I purchased a honeysuckle body lotion and mist. Jackson would answer with more than a buzz when I was around.

I arrived at the class a little bit earlier than usual wearing a golden brown pantsuit with a low cut blouse. Thankfully my feet were always smooth with my toes polished. The single strapped open toed shoes I wore showed that off. My hair was pulled into an upsweep with a swoop bang and the style accentuated my swan like neck. If he looked at me with the love I knew he would, he'd see how graceful every move I made was.

Jackson sat behind me and my body grew hot with his desire. I tried to sit poised, but the mere thought of him looking at me sent me into a mild hyper fit. When our first fifteen-minute break was announced I relaxed myself, and went, and stood in the hallway waiting for him to pass.

He approached me without his glasses.

"How are you this morning, Sherita? I wanted to greet you earlier but you seemed spellbound by our lesson."

We both smiled. If he only knew he was the reason for my inattentiveness...

"Me spellbound?" That's hardly the case. I have an event coming up that I have to prepare for. My mind was most likely on that." Jackson was that event.

Curiously, he asked, "Ah, so you're playing hooky in class. What made your mind stray?"

His voice sent waves of affection to me. I leaned in closer to him to inhale his scent. It was inebriating, intoxicating, exhilarating to the point that it made me babble.

"Uh, uh, oh, uh..."

He stood before me with a look that kissed me from afar. I was his without him asking. I had to find out about him. I had to know if he could freely be mine.

"I'm sorry, Jackson. It's just that your cologne smells so good. What are you wearing?"

"Thank you for noticing. It's a new cologne called Haven. I still can't put my finger on exactly what it smells like, but the sales clerk said it was very manly on me. I guess she was right."

Jealousy aroused in me at the thought of another woman adoring the smell on my man.

"Haven huh? I guess your woman will make sure you have plenty of that on hand."

His eyes traveled my body swiftly before he responded.

"Actually I'm single. But if the right woman comes along and likes this, I'll make sure I keep it in stock."

Jackson is single. Is he ready or even looking? Ask and you shall receive.

"So you're in the dating scene. That can be maddening at times."

"Well, I haven't dated much lately. I've been busy with work and these classes they keep springing on us. But believe me, I'm ready."

I was more than ready. He stood about six-foot-three and his frame would fit nicely in between my sheets and me.

Not one to let a good thing pass me by I asked, "Hey, umm, if I'm not being too forward would you like to get together sometime? I'm single as well and uh, well..."

My train of thought had left the station. I wanted to wrap my long silky legs around his torso and have him lift me up. Being near him felt secure. He could be my protector, my provider. He was the loving father to children, the herder to the sheep, and the lion to baby cubs. Jackson was what my existence had been missing.

"Sherita, I'm flattered. I'd love to go to dinner or dancing or do whatever it is you want to do," was his rushed reply.

In the seconds from my last thoughts to his words he put on his glasses. His acceptance of my offer came out like a dork that never had been on a date. He sounded like a nine-year-old boy who had mistakenly saw a breast in a nudie magazine. Was this the same man who had stolen my heart a minute ago? What kind of numbing power did his glasses have over me? Or was it him?

We were still standing in the hallway and I did something that only his hold over me would allow. I reached my hands up and removed his goggles. Those things had a fog around them. It prevented Jackson from being the exquisite man that my eyes had seen. He said nothing as I removed them and stared at him with erotic eyes.

"Why do you wear these all the time?" I lowered my voice and asked him in a hushed whisper.

"They're for reading, but I guess you know I can hide behind them."

"What are you hiding from?" I had to know.

"The hurt that I always receive from dysfunctional relationships."

"Who would hurt a beautiful man like you? You're too fine to hurt."

"A woman that can't see past my exterior."

With that I held my head. I was the type of woman he hid from. His glasses protected him from people like me.

"Jackson, I apologize. Give me a chance."

"I'd like nothing more than to get to know you, Sherita."

I gave him his eyeglasses back and this time when he put them on I still saw a black king. He walked with the same confident swagger, spoke with the same deep baritone, and moved like he knew how to please me.

We walked back into the class side by side and reclaimed our seats. My thoughts remained on him for most of the morning. We stole glances at each other and had our first date that afternoon for lunch. The three thousand seconds we spent on our lunch break were spent in found affection. I couldn't wait until the evening to see Jackson so I asked him to sit with me in my car. I had never done anything of the sort before. I drove to a closed off area of the lot and professed my feelings for the man that would be my new haven.

"Please don't think ill of me. It's just that you do something to me. I can't contain myself."

He didn't say a word as he removed his glasses.

"You, you don't have to take them off."

"Yes I do. They'll get in the way."

He then leaned in closer to me and pressed his lips into mine. My emotions ran wild. I placed my hands on each side of his face and massaged his velvet skin. He wrapped his arms around my back and moved them as if he were in a dance. His touch was delicate and I succumbed to him without worry.

"Jackson, I..."

He placed his finger over my mouth. I pulled it in kissing and sucking its delightful flavor.

"You're beautiful. I want you."

"Then take me."

He reached around me and let my seat fold back. Then he slid his seat back and reclined it, also. With soft controlled force he pulled me over on top of him and roamed my body with his hands. I had recently traded in my two-seater Mazda for a four-door model, which gave us a little more room to maneuver in.

We kissed and touched each other the same as a newly engaged couple. I couldn't get enough of him. I wanted him, but my first time with Jackson had to be extraordinary.

In between panting I managed to ask, "Can you come to my place after class?"

Without hesitation he said, "I thought you'd never ask."

We continued to please each other through our clothing. I could feel him and he felt superb. The man I needed lay beneath me, and my mind was abundant with thoughts on how to keep him there. Tonight at my place I'd make him want space to leave his things. The candlelight dinner would be roasted cherry glazed chicken tenderloins with asparagus tips, and parsley braised potatoes. We'd sip on a red merlot and undress each other before making it to the awaiting bubble bath. Tonight, Jackson would retire at a new address.

Knowing we had to get back to the afternoon portion of the class we composed and put ourselves back together. For the rest of the afternoon neither one of us could concentrate. We managed to remain professional, after all, this was our job, but the loving feelings that we displayed resonated throughout the class. The best part about it was that we didn't care. We wanted the world to know of our happiness.

At the end of the day Jackson walked me to my car. He didn't park next to me as he had done the previous day, so I drove him a few rows over to his car. He quickly hopped into his Taurus and followed me on the thirty-minute drive to my place. I pulled into my space and he parked behind me. He motioned for me to stay seated and then opened my car door and carried my study books up the two flights for me.

As we entered my place his hands lovingly roamed my back. He was such a comforter and put me at ease. I didn't care that I hadn't been with a man in awhile. He made me feel as if we had been together for years and that we had a connection that no one could ever break.

He sat my things down on the end of the sofa.

"Jackson, have a seat. Would you like a glass of wine?"

Through endearing eyes he answered. "Yes, but you have to join me."

"I will but only after I get started on dinner."

I heard him walking towards me. When I turned around he was standing directly in front of me.

"Sherita, we both did the same amount of work today. There is no way I'm going to sit here and let you make dinner. Let's order something in."

There were no words for me to respond with. He had become my man now, and I had to show him the many, many ways in which I would please him.

He wasn't wearing his glasses. "Put your glasses on, please."

I could tell he'd always satisfy me so he obliged without asking questions.

I began by removing his tie and unbuttoning his shirt. When it was open and hung freely from his body I slid it down his arms and let it fall to the floor. I removed my blazer as well. My nipples rose and showed themselves through my sheer blouse. He pulled my blouse over my head and unhooked my front clasp bra. My breasts sat perched high, waiting for him to do with them as he pleased. He bent a bit and took one into his mouth. I moaned and my knees buckled. He caught me as any sentinel would.

"Don't worry, Sherita. Relax, I'll always take care of you."

My lover had spoken. I listened to his gentle order and planned to follow it to the utmost.

As Jackson tantalized my chest I undid his belt and let his pants fall to the floor. He picked me up and stepped out of them. He held me wearing his boxers and dress socks.

"Walk down the hall and turn left." I gave him the directions to my bedroom. He took me there without missing a spot on my face, neck or chest with his lips. He placed me on my bed and took my pants, panties and knee-highs off in one slow seductive move. I lay before him naked with perspiration on the inside of my body fighting to get out. He took off his boxers and bent to take off his socks. When he returned upright I saw him as the man who would be my protector. His glasses complimented every ounce of his body—some ounces more than others.

My entire body opened up wide to receive him. We rose high and then low in our quest to find our safety zone. We found it with every move. With each thrust of our bodies came a welcomed release of our passionate fragrance to one another.

He moved with meticulousness and I held on with delight. I watched his glasses as he kissed me, as he moved me from within. They never faltered and only heightened my senses towards him. They took nothing away from his performance. As he went deep into my soul I cried out in pleasure, and spoke in a language only lovers can understand to show my appreciation.

We were married two years from the date of our first time together. Jackson continues to show my weak sighted eyes that he and his glasses were then and still are my new haven. They provide all of the customer service that I need and I never have to travel from home to receive it.

DSL

A stranger helped me carry my bags today. He didn't inquire about my name, or I his. He saw that I was struggling, and reached out to do everything humanly possible to assist me.

Actually, I saw this stranger's face two days ago. Our paths crossed as I was entering the subway station. He was exiting and didn't notice me as I stared at him head on. His sexy locs caught my eye. They were thick, neat, and the length would allow any amount of them to be grasped as he and I practiced making our first child together.

As usual, when I rode the train to work I'd read some type of romance novel that invited me into a world of my very own make-believe. This time my mind didn't wander in and out of the sentences. I became the character in the pages with the sexy loc man saving me from another long ride of gloom. Each time I felt myself becoming moist my eyes wandered the train quietly. This novel could become my screenplay if he were on board. Sexy locs could have seen me in his peripheral vision and come after me. I slowly slithered my eyes from left to right in hopes he followed me. I imagined that he found my beauty captivating and he had to have me. The fare of two dollars and fifty cents would be nothing to waste as he searched for the woman to make his wife. When my silent seated scavenger hunt ended with the sight of two women looking at me as if I were insane, my eyes returned to my book pages.

The next day the sexy loc stranger was mine. He approached me. The help he offered was his wish. Whatever else he had on his mind was put on hold without a second thought. I came first.

He quickened his stride and as he reached out to lend his masculine hands he said, "Here, let me help you with those." With one comforting swoop he removed most of the dangling bags from my hands.

My breathy reply was, "Thank you," and I huffed a bit as I speed up my pace to follow him.

As he walked up the stairs in front of me my eyes wandered to his derriere. It looked tight and firm, and would feel excellent with sections of it protruding between the slits of my fingers. At that moment, I wanted to lay with him.

It has been a long stretch for me. Sex didn't call my name anymore. No one did. Someone needed to connect to me in that way again. A man was missing. A man that would cater to me in every way imaginable. Only a man could power my desires up to the outside world. He could make my feelings come alive. He carried a remote for me that only contained an on switch. A man could enter me and channel surf. My body would turn on and become a wealth of information. My mind would be free of the simple thoughts that controlled it. The thoughts of seclusion, despair, and anxiety would flee once a man entered me. My legs would send a certain sensation. They'd extend and wrap snugly around the one that was sent to save me. My arms would reach out to pull him in closer; so close that our chests would draw an imaginary line between us. We'd connect like we were born for each other. My lips would become receptive to his tune and turn my body in to a pleasure palace. Sort of like DSL. A well-endowed man is my DSL.

"What's your apartment number, Miss?"

"1J. It's the first one on the right on the next floor."

We climbed another flight and I continued to view his backside. His complexion was mysterious and sinful, and his ass cheeks most likely looked the same, with the connection to his legs being a tad darker, but tasting just as delicious.

At the top of the stairs I gave a nod to the direction on my door. He moved over so I could insert the key into the hole, unlocking the place where my feelings have been held hostage. Our eyes met. He smiled as it clicked. DSL. Done...Slow...Long. That's what I wanted. It's what my body craved. DSL. Dick...So...Large. Ahh, the mere thought of him knocking the webs from my cave tempted me to take this chance meeting further.

The intense smell of passion fruit aroused our senses as we crossed the threshold. Candles burned in my place twenty-four hours a day, whether I was home or not. The fear of fire never entered my mind. If the flaming embers inside of me didn't set the place ablaze, nothing else would.

He spoke.

"Where would you like me to sit these?"

Tasty...delicious...sexy. I stood mesmerized in the moment. His lips were full and had the after effects of fresh saliva on them. Sexy locs. Saliva. He must have licked them. I wish I could have seen his tongue gliding over the entrance to his oral cavity. The urge to kiss him while he licked with seduction would have surely overpowered me. The man that stood in the entrance to my apartment didn't know how much power he held over me. I was weak. Weak from wanting him. Weak from waiting out a punishment I didn't deserve. This man would become my stay of execution at the thirteenth hour. He was the call I had been waiting for. He was the only man who had my number.

"The floor is fine. I don't want to put you through anymore trouble."

I lied. I wanted him to walk to my room and ooze into my bed like a body cream that would soothe my needing skin. Mama always told me not to lie, but then again, she's never seen a man worth lying for.

"Oh, it's no trouble at all. I live upstairs and was coming back home to get my cell phone. The timing was great."

Neighbor. It wouldn't be out of the ordinary to invite him over for a thank you dinner. No travel time to consider and in the morning, he could just trot back upstairs. That's if he spent the night. Oh, and he would stay the night.

"I've never seen you in the building before."

Stepping towards him I extended my hands for an embrace and hoped this would turn into a long rendezvous filled with pleasure.

"I'm Theresa Hilton. And you are?"

I raised the volume a bit on my silenced emotions. He reciprocated in kind.

"Damon LaBeer. I guess I should have said that before I accosted your groceries."

"No problem, Damon."

I grasped a hanging tendril off my face and twirled it in an alluring manner.

"So, have you lived in the building long?" My senses tingled at the thought of meeting him.

"Actually, no. I moved in two months ago. How long have you lived here?"

"Six years."

Six long years of solitude. Six long years of feening for a man to call my own. Six long years of unwanted celibacy.

"I guess you like it here, huh?"

"Yeah, it's okay. I'm single so I don't need much space."

I put my status out in one simple word. Hoping he'd latch on and ride, I continued.

"So, ah, are you single, also?"

His body language omitted signs of longing. I was an expert on certain things; isolation was my number one subject. He turned his head from side to side, as he roamed the floor looking for an inanimate object to meditate on. He was nervous for a reason. Damon was the first man who had been in my apartment that had been there just because. He wasn't there to read the meter, replace a lock, or overcharge me for jingling the lever on the toilet. That reason for his nervousness had to become me. He owned my thoughts when he said, "Yes, I'm single. When my girl and I called it quits I moved here."

Instantly his eyes returned to the floor. They traveled my bags possibly for an invitation to sample their contents.

"Hey, how about staying for dinner? It's 5:32 now and I'd like some company. Look at it as a friendship offering or payment for carrying my bags."

"Thank you, Theresa. I haven't had a home cooked meal in months. I was on my way to the video store, but this offer is much better."

Smiles came from the both of us. It seemed to take up only a centimeter of our time but it was filled with a design for our lives.

"Good. Have a seat on the sofa. How does spaghetti and meatballs sound?"

"One of my favorites. Thanks for the invite."

Before he turned to walk away he asked, "Do you need any help?"

My movements mimicked a slow, sexy, hair shampoo commercial. Through my fumbled actions, my eyes landed on his delicious thick neck, as I replied, "No, Sir. Go ahead and get comfortable. The remote for the TV is on top of the stand. You make yourself at home while I get started."

Damon smiled and sauntered his way to the sofa. He walked with a slow subtle pimp that held mystery. His legs were slightly bowed, and his stride was peaceful. My mind raced with the visuals of him coming home from work to me. I'd greet him at the door with a kiss. As I tried to pull away he'd want more and we'd give our neighbors a peep show of our love. Some days Damon would pick me up and carry me over the threshold, signaling his effort to keep our love new.

Our wedding would be magnificent. The entertainment channels, the rich and famous and even a few dignitaries would all hanker for an invitation to the affair of the decade. All of this came from a simple connection. A simple connection called DSL.

While I got started on our meal humming a low tune, my face became hot. I forgot about the porno tape that was still lodged in my VCR from the night before. I hadn't watched TV at all today and it was still set on *HUNG 2008.* The closest I'd come in the last six years to seeing the member of the male anatomy that was created for a woman was on a tape. It didn't matter if it was VHS or DVD. I owned them all. The tape that greeted Damon was Triple X Rated. Hurriedly, I grabbed a couple of glasses and a corkscrew, a bottle of wine, and rushed into the living room. It was too late. Damon's eyes met mine.

Sincerely I said, "I'm sorry." His gaze went from the TV to my face a few times. The time frame that elapsed was long in its short seconds. I continued. "Here, take these and I'll take care of that."

When he took the contents for our mood setting from my hands, I felt him staring at me. His words came to me in slow motion. They had the aura of sex intertwined.

"Are you embarrassed?" he asked with concern.

Meekly I replied, "Yes. Shouldn't I be?"

"No." *Ahh, my knight in shining armor.* "Everybody watches porn. Don't worry about it. I even have a few tapes upstairs."

Damon began uncorking the wine bottle. He worked it with ease. He'd use that same ease as he entered me.

"Maybe we can watch them together one day."

Our eyes met again. DSL. Direct...Service...Link. Damon carried the link that would directly service me. I cleared my throat before responding.

"You want to watch porn with *me*? That's something that's done between lovers...not people like us."

His face scrunched a bit and his sexy lips rippled. His lips were thick and dark pink. Sexy lips that would send my body into intense shivers. Lips that would leave subtle wet kisses down my spine. Mine could easily suck his lips. I'd nibble them and lick away any throbbing feeling I left.

"*People like us?* Please...elaborate."

Knowing he held my tongue in his hands, he sat back on the sofa momentarily. Then, he seductively leaned forward and poured our wine the same as a skilled bartender. A taste of it splashed on his finger and he licked it off erotically before handing me my glass. He was devastatingly wonderful. It would kill me not to have him, if only for a short while.

My insides were flustered the same as a goldfish that had flipped out of its bowl. I lifted my glass to my lips in an attempt to look mysterious.

"I thought most people watch stuff like this with people they're close to. Not people who are just getting to know one another."

I lay my glass on my mouth so it would only tease the surface. My face searched his for some sort of agreement. He said nothing as he sipped his liquid soother.

Taking a swig was supposed to calm my nerves. It didn't, so I continued.

"Do you have a different opinion?" was my nervous reply.

For the first time I noticed how endearing Damon's eyes were. They searched my body up and then down, slowly, as if he wanted what I had. His tongue traced the rim of the glass before he sat it down. I held my breath and then let it out in short bursts, waiting for his reply.

"Look, maybe this was a bad idea. I'll see you around, okay?"

Panic! No! Those words were not correct! I'm here for you. I'm your outlet. Plug into me. DSL.

He didn't notice me as he stood to leave. If he did, he would have seen the pangs of wanting that I displayed. Foolishly, I made him feel self-conscious by not being more truthful. Once again I lied; I wanted to watch the tape with him. He was a total stranger but he had what I needed.

"Damon wait, please don't leave. If you want to watch the tape, it's cool. I don't mind."

My heart quivered as I watched him. He took two steps towards me and kissed me on the cheek. Moist. Tempting. Passion. I felt all of these from one simple kiss.

"Theresa, how about we exchange numbers and hook up later? Ahh...I don't want you to feel uncomfortable in your own home."

Beg. Beggar. Begging.

"Okay. I understand. Can you call me tonight?"

Desperate women ask questions in desperation. I shifted and shuffled my legs hoping he'd say of course, there's no one else in the world I'd rather talk to. He said nothing. I was relentless in my pursuit of him. When the sun came up in the morning is when he would leave.

"Damon, I'm not uncomfortable. Really, I'm not. Are you? Is that why you're leaving?"

In the act of...in motion. Begging is what fit best.

"Truthfully, no. I've been celibate for three years now. My ex kept pressuring me to have sex. I decided that I would only have sex with the woman I married."

Amazement stifled me. A man who thought the same as I? Damon was the man sent for me. My morals weren't being compromised. Electricity consumed my body. The shock waves engaged him. This was the plan. It would come to pass. I had to have him.

"In my opinion porno movies are just bad movies with sex scenes to me."

He saw that my voice was silenced and after a brief pause he said, "Look, I'm a first time guest in your home. You tell me what to do."

Sexual thoughts ran rampant through my mind. They came to me fast, and then slow, hot, and then cold. My brow beaded with sweat as my nipples hardened. For him I didn't mind becoming a whore. But what if he declined my offer? He had ended a relationship because of his morals, his values. He was sent here to have sex with me. We are going to make love. We're of the same mind. He has to know that. Was I becoming a fool because of lack of sex?

"Theresa, are you okay?"

I wanted this luscious man.

"I'm fine."

I have to taste him.

"Damon, I know you're going to leave after this but I have to say it. I haven't had sex in the last six years. I'm about to burst. I want you."

"Theresa, I can't."

Beggar...one that begs.

"Please."

Damon stepped towards me. He took my hands gently into his and raised them up to his lips.

"You're beautiful. Since we're being honest I have to tell the truth. I saw you three weeks ago. You were down on 183rd Street. It looked as if you had just come off the subway. I followed you. When I saw you enter this building I began semi-stalking you. I watched the entrance door for you. Today was partly planned. I have dreams about you every night. I want you, too."

My coyness left me totally then. Damon and I leaned in towards one another and our lips met. I pushed my tongue into his mouth in a shameless manner, which was rough, but I made my point. He knew he could handle me. Time heals all wounds. Six years of being alone was mended with a kiss.

The sheer tee I wore had a light bra sewn into it. It did nothing to conceal my enlarged heaving breasts. Damon pulled me closer to him. Our bodies relaxed but stood tall at the same time. I felt him as I spread my legs. The blue linen slacks he wore helped his erectness ease between them. It stayed there. It was home; in a soothing location that belonged to him.

I stepped away from him.

"Come to my bedroom." I said this with my voice, my eyes and my body.

Already knowing the layout of my apartment Damon led the way. He gently caressed my hand as he led me to our place of consummation. The place where we'd cohabitate and become one suddenly came alive. My bed seemed as if it had arms that extended outward to greet Damon and I as we approached. The sheets slid back on their own, while the lights dimmed to an enthralling tone and set the mood for our venture.

We faced each other when we reached the bed. Damon spoke.

"If we do this there will be no turning back. You have to become mine."

His eyes pierced though my soul when I heard his words.

"Damon, I have nothing to turn back to. You are the man I need. You have what I crave."

Our tryst continued with him removing my clothing with his hands, his teeth and his lips. Ahh, the feel of those thick lips. DSL. I ran my hands through his locs. Thick lips. Thick sexy locs. A well maintained body. I loved all the options that were included. My DSL Package was complete.

It was hard for me not to faint as he nibbled my stomach down to my toes. I fought back screams of enjoyment. Excitement, the same as the victor on the movie screen receiving her due. DSL. I experienced this because of a connection to DSL. The urge to have him answer my prayers came over me.

I was naked and my body temperature was boiling. Beads of moisture raced down my spine and held in the curve of my back, waiting to be massaged in by manly hands.

"Damon, tell me your middle name..."

His face was directly in front of mine. His hands had traveled my nude frame back up and he rubbed me from the inside out. I wanted to say more, but his sweet tongue dove into my mouth. I lowered my tongue and let him take control of the place where my vocal feelings could escape.

He ran his hands around my face and up into my hair. He twirled my curls tightly within his fingertips. As his tongue wove deeper and deeper into my soul he grasped them hard, pulling me closer to him, owning all that I had to offer.

Damon released me gently and lifted one knee as he guided me down on the bed. He used the same knee to guide himself as he came in for a perfect landing on top of me. Before he hit his mark he said, "Steven," and with that, I exploded.

His arms went under my legs and they were pushed up to the headboard. I spread them wide and felt the tip of Damon's erotic gift to me. He was at least nine inches of smooth, hard splendor.

He entered me slow. His rhythm was the same as a serenading jazz musician. It was haunting, quiet, soothing. Excellence had entered me. Damon Steven LaBeer had saved me. His touches were methodical, calculated, still. My breathing halted within his every sense. I inhaled his aroma. He drew me in. My life became his leisure. I panted. The room was hot, hell hot. Our sweat glistened and reflected off of one another's body. We licked each other, tasting the delicious quencher each of our souls poured out.

As our bodies thrust upward I moaned. The ecstasy filled sounds came fast. Then faster, then quickened to the velocity of racing thoughts. I screamed, as I grew closer to my sensation,

"D!"

Damon kissed my neck and embedded his face there.

"S!"

He held me tighter, gripping my ass, my back, and my life with his body.

"L!"

The release was magical. I felt every ounce he offered and took it as if he had stolen it from me. It was mine. It belonged to me. Over and over in my mind I chanted, DSL, DSL, DSL. He opened me up to a new world. With one turn of a driver he made me a woman.

Exhilarating seconds passed and he asked, "Theresa, are you okay?" Damon kissed me deeply before I could answer. He stayed inside of me but slid his body down to see my face full on.

"Are you okay," he asked again.

"Yes. That was exquisite. I, uh, I hope I didn't make to much noise." I was a bit embarrassed of my barbaric behavior but I couldn't control myself.

"Your voice turns me on. Everything about you turns me on. Theresa Hilton. The woman that will be mine forever."

We stared at each other a few more moments before I felt him growing inside of me. He slid his body back up and began to make me feel as if I were the first and only woman he'd ever loved. He squeezed my breasts and drew a sensation from me that I don't ever recall feeling. A bed of love, locs, and lips. I closed my eyes and saw brilliance. Damon was dark mocha. My complexion was vanilla cappuccino. The two mixed together was sinfully fulfilling. He dispensed his color deep into mine. We worked together blending a mix that didn't need a taste test nor would a power outage shut down our connection.

"Damon, ahh, Damooon…oh, yes."

DSL. Some say it's too expensive for the service failures that come along with it. I will honestly attest to the fact that my personalized service will never fail me. The remote will never need batteries. By the simple graze or mere touch of my hand it will do whatever I command.

"Ahh, Damooon….oh, yes."

"That's it, baby. Say your man's name."

"DSL…DSL…DSL…"

I exploded many times that evening with each time more intense than the first. The plug that enticed my world was drenched with sweet nectar that kept it stoking. Six years of juice that waited to flow came down a magnificent channel. Six years of celibacy had led me to my loving man. Many times I could have chosen cable with over 200 stations, but this connection was everlasting. This program was here to say. I'd never change the channel on my DSL.

Work the Stick in My Ride

"The Army? Linda, are you serious? I can't believe what I'm hearing. *You* want to join the Army as a truck driver? Wait, don't say another word until I sit down."

"Oh, please! Give me a break. I told you that I was joining the service after High School."

Hugging her sides and doubling over in laughter was the first part of April's response. When she was able to compose herself enough to speak she said, "Ha, ha, ha, ha! Whew, Linda. You are hilarious. Your old ass has been out of school for twelve damn years! Give *me* a break. Tell me the truth. What's this really about?"

April and I have been best friends since we met at her cousin's sixteenth birthday party. I was her cousin's date, but I really wanted her brother. She put a plan in motion for him and I to dance, and we have been inseparable ever since.

"Tsk. You think you know me so well don't you?"

Sarcastically April replied, "Bitch, just start yapping."

Where does she get the nerve to sit on my couch eating greasy potato chips *and* call me a bitch in the same crunch with crumbs spilling out of her mouth? She'd better be glad that I love her.

"Quit daydreaming, Linda. What are you up to? Oh, before you begin, can you get me some of that cheap ass soda you buy? These chips are dry."

While I walked into the kitchen my mind began to rumble. I had to tell someone of my plans and a best friend was the best place to start.

"I'm bored with my life. I want a change. My job as a sales clerk is just too tedious for the pay. The Army seems so exciting. I'd see the world for free, and get trained to do a job without sending out resumes."

I handed her the glass and she took a long gulp before she replied. "Fool, we're at war. They will send your ass too. Have you even considered that?"

"Of course I thought about that." Actually, I hadn't. "But there are many women there already. And the training would always come in handy and I'd meet so many people."

April smirked. "Yeah, that's fine, but as soon as you sign your name on the dotted line and raise your right hand you're outta here. Instead of you driving, you'd probably get a scud missile driven up your ass. Wait, don't sit down, can I get a refill?"

Rolling my eyes I responded, "You make me sick."

Surrendering to her feelings, she backed off a bit.

"Okay, okay. I see this means a lot to you, but listen. You're my ace. I'd miss you for one, and two, well; I just don't want you to do this. I really think you should reconsider."

April and I sat in silence pondering other avenues for me to take. When a brilliant plan came her face lit up.

"Hey! Why don't you get a CDL and drive for a company around here? You'll get your change, meet new people and stay here in the process."

Nodding swiftly and grinning I agreed with her option.

"You are so right. Shoot, my tail is too old to get through basic training, and the thought of firing a gun is terrifying. I thought I had to go away to do something drastic. You know doing things on impulse have always been my problem."

"What in the world would you do without me?"

Not wanting to view April's gloating of me I hopped up and stomped into the kitchen like a scolded child. She and I burst out laughing, and I had to compose myself before pouring her another tall glass of flat orange soda. April wiped the laughter tears from her eyes as I walked back into the living room, and sat her glass down next to her.

"I'm really serious about making a change. After work Monday I'll go to the DMV and get the study guide. Having no money and no man is starting to get old."

April folded the chip bag as she spoke. "Ahhh, so that's what this is about. You're looking for a man aren't you? The Army would be a good place for that."

Pacing and twirling my hair in frustration I continued, "Girl, TJ and I are through. The mama's boy bull was cute in the beginning but I am so sick of it. Do you know his mama called here the other night at three a.m. talking about a leaking faucet?"

"What? Now that's just ridiculous."

"That's not the half of it. TJ got his ass up and went to her house. I know she was calling for another female. I'm still boiling about that shit."

"Umph. Sounds like you do need an upgrade."

Suddenly I had an energy that pulsed through my veins. "Yes I do. You know, I could join the Y for the exercise aspect and try to drive for Division Parcel Service. I saw an ad for them in the paper a few days ago. What do you think?"

"I think that's a plan, girl. Highway 55 better watch out!"

Telling my feelings to April was the best thing to do. If I didn't say anything I probably would've joined the Army and been miserable.

"How about we go to the DMV today before you change your mind? Its 2:30 and they don't close until four p.m."

"Uh, *we?*"

April tried to contain her smile but it was a bit too big for her jaws. "I'm going to make sure you do this. I don't want you leaving me."

That's my girl. We quickly put up her snack food and ran out the door. We both worked a half-day and still had on our store uniforms. It was a Friday afternoon and we planned to go to happy hour at the corner bar for the watered down drink specials, cold hot wings, and men that would make any woman celibate.

April drove my car and we arrived at the Department of Motor Vehicles ten minutes later. The lot was usually full but today it was empty. The few cars parked near the entrance were most likely the employees, and there were only about ten other ones scattered about.

"This is your lucky day. We got here in record time, and it doesn't seem to be crowded. I'll wait here for you."

"Alright. I'll be right back," I eagerly replied.

I stepped out of my car feeling that I was doing the right thing to add a little spice to my life. Through the glass doors I could see that the building was partially empty, and a very handsome male was stationed behind the service counter. There were two people standing in the line waiting and I hurried over to become number three.

"Next customer please." The service clerks voice was very mellow but deep. His command flowed from his lips soft, but in a masculine tone. Wanting to jump over the counter and rip his clothes off was the urge I suppressed as the first person in line turned to the next and said,

"You can go ahead of me, lady. I'm waiting for my wife." It truly was my lucky day because the woman turned to me and said,

"You go ahead, Miss. I have to fill out the rest of this renewal form."

With a polite thank you and a beaming smile, I stepped around the two patrons and glided to the desk. As I drew nearer to the service clerk, his cologne pulled me into his atmosphere, silently lulling me into a lustful world.

"Hello, Miss. How can I help you?"

Suddenly, my tongue went numb and the reason for my visit to the DMV was forgotten. My eyes took in the clerks face for a few seconds before I lowered them to his nametag, and returned them back to his lips, where they stayed still until he repeated his question.

"Uh, excuse me, Miss. How may I help you?"

"Oh, uh, I'm sorry. You caught me daydreaming. I'd like to get information on obtaining a Commercial Driver's License. Am I in the right place?"

"Yes, you are. Here, this is the manual. It contains all the information you need. Can I help you with anything else?"

Before answering, I thumbed through the manual trying to find a tidbit to strike up a conversation.

"Uh, I don't want to sound like a "female driver," but what do they mean by clutch and shifting gears?"

The service clerk smiled and shook his head slightly before responding. "Those terms are associated with a vehicle that is standard shift. It's nothing to worry about if you can drive a standard shift."

I was a little puzzled but remained cool and nonchalantly answered my own question. "Standard shift? Oh, I get it, a stick right?"

"Yes a stick. Do you know how to drive a standard shift?"

My face changed to innocence. "No. Is it mandatory for a CDL?"

I'd swear his chest puffed up. "No, not really. However, if you want to learn how to drive the big rigs it would come in handy. Many trucks have clutches, gears, and things of that nature. Not knowing how to drive a standard shift may stop you from getting work one day, but I'm not an expert."

Scott, that's what his nametag read, had the plumpest lips I've ever seen on a man. His breath smelled of sweet juicy fruit and I wished I could run my tongue across his. The goal of changing careers was still first, but getting Scott in on the action would be a major plus.

"Hmmm. Listen, you seem to be very knowledgeable on the subject. Do you know how to drive a stick?"

"I sure do," Scott happily said.

Wonderful. "Well, would you like to teach me? I'm a quick learner and I'll pay you whatever you want."

Scott put down the notepad he held and curiously asked, "Are you serious?"

"I've never been more serious in my life. I've been driving for sixteen years and have a clean record. Come' on, don't be bashful. I won't hurt you."

"Okaaaay. Let's start from scratch. What's your name?"

Haste took over. "Linda Hart. So how about it? Are you in?"

Scott contemplated my request and looked around the room for a few moments before responding. "Sure. You seem enthusiastic and I'd love to help you. Besides, I taught my mother and my sister. There's no way you can be worse than them."

Scott and I laughed as he wrote his phone number and address down for me.

"Here you go, Linda. I'm available all day tomorrow. Give me a call, okay?"

"How's three p.m.? I'll even buy you dinner."

"Ah, a woman after my own wheels. I'll see you tomorrow."

"Thanks, Scott. Have a good evening. Bye."

"You too, Linda. Bye."

Scott and I shook hands and I felt like a swan ballerina floating away. The two other customers gave me snide looks for taking so long, so I mouthed an apology, and continued out the door. When my hand pulled the handle to my car April reminded me why she can get on my nerves.

"Damn, Linda! What the fuck took so long? You know we have to get ready for happy hour!"

Killing her with kindness always worked. I sat in the seat and gave a pleasing smile. She was still tight as she started the car.

"What happened in there?"

"April, I have a date with a DMV worker named Scott tomorrow. He's going to teach me how to work the stick in my ride."

Quickly she turned the car off. "What? What the hell do you mean stick in your ride? We're not moving until you explain."

Telling April what happened between Scott and I took less than two minutes. She interrupted me twice but I spoke over her and left no details out.

"Linda! You are so nasty! You're not thinking about a damn stick in a car are you?"

"Girl, I don't know what's gotten into me. I've never got down with a guy the first time we hooked up. I can't wait to see what his stick looks like."

"Dang, you sound like a whore."

"What's so wrong with that?"

April and I burst out with loud guffaws and mild choking in between. At her cousin's sixteenth birthday, I bed her brother in the downstairs basement, and April reminded me of it as we laughed.

"I hope you don't make his nose bleed like you did Ricky's. You had my brother smelling you from miles away."

"If he can put it down like I think he can…"

"Uh, oh. He'd better watch out. Hey, do you want me to tag along for encouragement?"

Cutting my eyes at her was the only gesture she needed. She laughed, started the car, and we talked about what I should wear when I saw Scott the next day.

We didn't stay out late that Friday night because all I could focus on was Scott. The next morning I awoke at seven and went for a brisk walk. When I came back home I took a nice long bubble bath, fingering myself for a more sensuous effect, and imagined how the afternoon would go.

At 2:40 p.m. I called him to tell him I was on my way.

"Hello?"

"Hey, Scott. It's me, Linda. I'm coming over now if you haven't changed your mind. You ready?"

"Hi, Linda. I thought about you all night long. No, I haven't changed my mind and yes I'm ready. I have an older car that I use to train people with. It just sits in the garage when I'm not using it. I just came in from sprucing it up."

Lovely. "Ah, is that where our lesson will begin?"

"Yes. We'll go over the fundamentals and maybe even hit the road. I'm going to taker a shower now, okay. I'll see you in a few."

"Okay. See ya soon."

The telephone rang but instead of answering it and prolonging my sexual escapade by talking to April, I bound out the door the same as a team of sled dogs that were desperate to maintain their lead.

Scott lived twenty minutes away but it seemed like my ride took over an hour. I pulled up in his driveway and he greeted me with a hug as I exited my car.

"Hey. Would you like something to drink before we get started?"

"No, I'm fine. I ready to learn this stick thingy."

Laughing he replied, "Okay then, follow me."

I trailed Scott and his musk scent into his well-kept garage. His backside was very muscular and I had to hold my hands together to stop myself from slapping his ass cheeks.

"Alright, Linda. We'll begin our lesson with you on the driver's side. Let me open the door for you."

My body brushed up against Scott's before I sat in the seat. He was hard all over.

"Scott, what kind of car is this? I've never been in something so compact."

"It's a Toyota MR2. It was the thing to have when they first came out in the 80's. I guess I felt like a part of Miami Vice with the two seats. It's old, but I just don't have the heart to get rid of it."

"Men. You guys are so sentimental about your cars."

"Hey, on a lonely night they come in handy."

When Scott said that he placed his hand on mine. His hand was smooth and could caress and cling to my body the same as cashmere.

"Okay, Linda. First, you have to familiarize yourself with the controls. There's more to driving a standard shift than just shifting."

"I see. You didn't say anything about there being three pedals to press."

Assuring me he said, Oh don't worry. You'll get the hang of that in no time."

Not wanting to seem blunt, I slid my hands around the steering wheel for a few minutes before making my move to why I was really there.

"So, this black thing is the stick?"

"Yes it is. Go ahead. Touch it."

I reached my hand over and slid it up and down the firm handle in a slow, rhythmic movement. Scott grew silent as he watched me tease the tip of it. His breathing heightened when I returned my hand to the up and down movement. Fondling it as if it were something so real and so wonderful.

"Scott, am I doing it right? Is this how you work a stick?"

He cleared his throat and fidgeted in his seat. "Uh huh. You have the hang of it. It looks like you're a pro."

Cunningly, I asked, "Would you like me to show you exactly how much I know?"

Wanting to know what I meant Scott said, "Oh, uh, sure."

Keeping my same rhythm, I moved my hand over to Scott's groin area and continued the movements on him. The thin pair of linen slacks he wore didn't hide his erection as I worked my hand on his stick a little faster.

My eyes seductively met his. "Why don't you pull it out so I can get a better grip?"

He didn't say a word as he unzipped his pants, raised his body up off the seat, and pulled his pants and boxers down to his knees. His stick stood rigid and it was splendid.

"Uhm, this is very nice. Linda, you're an excellent pupil."

"Why thank you. I still have so much to learn. Instruct me please."

"Ahh, okay, its time for you to shift gears. Coming out of neutral is tricky. Move the stick a little to the left and down, and then work the shaft a little bit faster."

I followed Scott's instructions to a tee as he moaned with delight.

"Mmmm, wow, you're good at this. Okay, let's put it in second. Move it a bit forward and speed up the shaft movement."

Scott gave his instructions in a lusty, fantastic tone. I had him right where I wanted him.

"Ooh, ooh. We can skip third gear. Move the stick back and work in the two lower round gears on the down stroke. Ahh, in fourth gear the stick has the control."

The paisley skirt I wore had risen up past my knees and settled in on my thighs. My body was dripping and ready to take off on a speedway, going one hundred miles over the limit.

"Scott, how many gears are there?"

"This car only has five. I'm ready to go to the fifth gear. Are you ready for your instructions?"

My breathing had quickened and I swallowed before I responded. "Yes. Oh, yes. Tell me how to get to fifth gear."

"Ahh, ooh. We can only get to fifth gear when you use another instrument to work the stick. That's the only way we will be able to move."

Although the car was a two-seater Scott and I had plenty of room to maneuver. We both moved our seats as far back as they would go and I swung my left leg over his body. He helped me balance myself by holding my slender waist, and sliding his frame down lower in his seat.

"Oh…I'm ready to drive."

I stood five-feet even and was able to place the soles of my feet on either side of Scott on the seat. My hands were on his headrest and I lowered myself cautiously onto his stick. Not wearing panties was part of my plan and it worked the same as Armor All on wheels - immaculate.

"Yes, the stick needs lubrication. Ooh, you are oiling it up very well. Ahh, this ride will run very smooth."

"Uh, huh. Yes it will," I said in agreement.

Scott's stick was very large, long and wide. Once I took all of him in, we moved systematically in precision, switching gears and downshifting from fast to slow without losing speed.

"Linda, you're the best student I've ever had. Oh, damn you know how to work a stick. Oh."

My entire body hummed and I couldn't answer Scott. I sounded the same as a vehicle that had been tuned. Not one piston or belt pulsated out of time.

He could barely speak. "We have to slow it down now. It's time for us to go back to first gear. The engine is about to blow."

"Okay, okay. Let's downshift. I'm ready."

We maintained our well-oiled machine for about twenty-five minutes before I stopped my shifting of his stick, and sat still and upward as he filled me up with his lubricant. My chest met his when he was finished, and I listened to him grade me on my driving performance.

"You get an A+ for this lesson. I thought you didn't know how to drive a standard shift. You were excellent."

Satisfied but wanting more I slyly asked, "So, will you give me another lesson? This time we can use my car, though."

Smirking with relief Scott said, "I thought you didn't have a stick? Besides, there isn't a thing I can teach or show you. What else do you think I know?"

"Well, with you in my car it will become a standard shift," I said with much enthusiasm. "And before I can drive it I'll need to be taught how to work the stick in my ride."

This Rhythm Is Rated L

Damn, I can't wait for Sheree to get here. That girl has got me wide open. I've never felt anything like I do for her. That sexy slow hip swinging walk, her seductive take all of me smile, and that make me do whatever she wants voice will drive anyone wild.

The first time I saw her she was working the afternoon shift at a downtown L train ticket booth. I'd heard about her from friends at work and was told she was way out of my league. Still, I wanted to get to know her and asked for advice from a friend of a friend of hers.

"Hey, Lance, you know the girl who works at the L train booth? The one that's usually there when we get off work?"

"Yeah, that tight pretty girl? I wouldn't mind hittin' that. What about her?"

"Tell me about her. Is she single, married, you know, stuff like that."

"Is this information for you?"

Lance turned his face up when he responded and that irritated me. I was just as good as he was and would treat a woman better than she'd ever imagine.

"Yes the information is for me. Do you have a problem with that? Are you trying to get with her?"

"No, no. I just think she may be a bit much for you. I mean, look at her."

A stern solemn look showed Lance that I was serious.

"I do look at her. That's why I want to get to know her. Are you going to give me any information or not?"

"I didn't mean it like that. I just took you to be more settled and reserved that's all. I've heard a few things about her and well..."

"Is she married?"

"She's single, but loose."

"You know this for a fact? Did she tell you this?"

"No, but men talk. I heard she'd do anything for the right price. You sure you want to get with her? As fine as she is I wouldn't mind, but I'm not paying."

Lance was a ladies man and could probably pull any woman he chose. I'd never put myself down, but I wasn't flashy and did have a hard time approaching women. This time things would be different though. Sheree was too fine to not try for.

"I have to take a chance on this one. Maybe I'll be just what she needs. I'll keep you posted."

"Well good luck. Let me know if I can be of any service. You know how I get down."

"Thanks but no thanks. I want this to last."

Lance laughed and patted me on the back as he left. The only way I'd take advice from him is if I wanted to be single forever.

That day I'd speak to Sheree. Although I never placed myself close enough to talk she was always in my view. I couldn't take my eyes off of her. Her hazelnut colored skin complemented her light brown eyes. She had a set of lips that a collagen injection couldn't obtain and they were glossed up beautifully. Even the cornrows going down her back were fine.

I purchased a metro card from a machine and pretended it didn't work. The window could have been broken with the way I almost went through it trying to get to her. She easily saw through my attempt to woo her and knew she had all of me at that moment. She gave an "I'm game" vibe and played along with me.

"It seems you're having problems with your metro card that works just fine. Now what is it you really want, my number?"

"Uh, yeah. If you don't mind."

"Why don't you give me a few good reasons why I should reveal my digits to you? What makes you so special?"

I knew many reasons that would make her proud to be with me but couldn't think of any at that moment.

"Well, I'm waiting. What's up?"

My mind went into a mild trance and I had a vision of my tongue licking her all over her body. I couldn't wait to taste every orifice she had from the inside out. A tired line like, "Heaven must be missing an angel," almost came out. Thank God someone needing a token saved me.

"Would you kindly step aside while you think of something to say? My line is getting long."

Sheree placed a sly grin on her face while giving a sexy don't go anywhere look. That girl knew I wouldn't move until she told me to. I aggravated many customers because I only moved over slightly. It wasn't enough for anyone to completely pass by without bumping me. I didn't care; Sheree was going to be my lady starting today.

After the line cleared I stepped back in front of the booth with a head and heart full of reasons as to why we should become one. Rambling them off without breathing caused her to smile and got me her number in the process.

"I'm not a poet or anything but you're a beautiful woman. Just give me a chance, let me take you to dinner, a movie, or just go for a walk. I work hard and can give you everything you need. I don't play games and never mess around. Just give me a chance."

Sheree eyed me up and down, no doubt trying to take me in. I stepped back from the booth so she could see all I had to offer. I'd just gotten off work and looked presentable in my dress down Friday casual shirt and pants. Our eyes met a few times as I eyed her in return. Although she had on a uniform shirt I could see her ample sized breasts through it. She had to be a thirty-four C cup. Uhmm, I had to get a grip of them and myself. I opened my mouth slightly, imagining I had her nipple there and began caressing my crotch. A seductive smile on Sheree's face informed me that she'd be sweet.

Sheree didn't say anything as she handed me her number. As I took it our hands touched. Her hand was soft and I squeezed it as best as I could through the window opening. Touching her aroused me and she knew it. She placed her other hand on top of mine and blew me a kiss. She then told me to call her and said bye. I stared at her for a few more moments before walking off and then turning to wave. Sheree didn't notice me, though. Some woman was talking to her as if they were best friends. It was then that I vowed to make her mine.

Calling Sheree as soon I got home was the only thing on my mind. She wasn't there so I left a message with my number hoping that she'd call me. I left the same message for the next two weeks and she never called. The closest I could get to her was seeing her at the ticket booth, which I did everyday. The day I saw her on the outside of the booth was the day I began sending her flowers and cards. The shape this girl had was incredible. Along with her breasts she had a small huggable waist that flared into thick hips and shapely thighs. Her ass was a round enticing hook that grabbed me at first sight. That girl must drink gotdayum juice. The only words that came from me were gotdayum over and over. She looked to be about five-feet-five and that was right on time. I stood five-foot-seven so we'd make the perfect couple.

The third time I sent her flowers she called. Trying to smell her through the phone caused me to panic, and I had an orgasm when she said she'd come over after work.

"Hey, Sheree, how are you?"

I tried to sound collected, but the sweat coming from my pores wouldn't let me.

"Fine. I just called to say thanks for the flowers and stuff. I guess I haven't given you much attention. I think I know how to make it up to you. What'cha doin' later?"

Yes. "Nothing. What's up?"

"I'm coming by your place after work. What's your address?"

"Nine-Thirty East Ninth Street, apartment 3-C. What time should I expect you?"

"Eager aren't we? That's good. I'll be there around eleven. I hope you're worth the trip."

Sheree hanging up before I could answer sent me into overdrive. Quickly, I jumped up and gave my place a once over, with the first thing being changing the sheets on the bed, and placing candles around the room. She wanted me, and would I give me to her better than anyone before had ever done. Less than an hour remained before she'd arrive, and I hopped in the shower while listening to a combination of Teddy P, Johnny Gill and the Isley Brothers. When Between The Sheets came on I knew this night would go smoothly.

The doorbell rang at 11:02 and my body tensed. I ran to the door panting and swung it open. Beauty stood before me wearing a low cut, thigh high, blue dress. Her open toe ankle strapped sandals revealed her French pedicure. She wasted no time in stepping past me and dropping her belongings on the floor. Dress included.

I closed the door and faced Sheree. We smiled as I disrobed. We stepped towards each other and our breasts touched. Feeling her made my nipples hard and she reached her hands up to caress them. I moaned and pulled Sheree closer to me. My hands moved all around her body trying to touch her all at once. When our lips met I fell in love. She continued to kiss my neck and face before I led her into the last bedroom she'd need.

She winded for me while she lay on the bed. My eyes gazed her beautiful waving body up and down. I wanted to go fast and slow so I sucked her nipples and fingered her at the same time. When I began my journey to her waxed vagina she stopped me.

"Sheree, what's wrong? Am I doing something you don't like?"

"No, Tammy, you're good. The tongue is the appetizer, but I need to know what I'm getting for the main course. Do you have a strap on?"

"No, but I can make up for it other ways."

"No? Make up for it how? Your fingers aren't long or fat enough. Do you have any friends that have one or can come over?"

"Sheree," pleading was all I could do, "I want you to be my girl forever, not just tonight. I don't want to share you."

"Look, you're cute and all that but I want a total package woman. Is this your first time or something?"

"No."

"How many women have you had?"

"One."

Sheree sucked her teeth in disgust. She sat up and swung her feet over me and off the bed. My eyes filled with tears because I didn't know what to say to make her stay.

"You're damn near a virgin. When I need to be pleased I want it done right. I'm nobody's practice. Call me in a few months. Maybe we can hook up then."

"Wait, wait a minute. Let's talk and I'll cook you something. Please don't leave."

She never responded with words, just movements that showed me she wouldn't be my bedmate tonight. Like a stray dog I followed Sheree as she walked out the room and put her clothes on. She said nothing more as she walked out the door, slamming it behind her.

A strap on? My last girl, Dana, told me I was too timid. She said since I was a woman I should know how to touch and please one just right. Sheree had to come to me again - I'd do anything to be with her once more.

I went into my room and lay on the bed in Sheree's spot. My face crashed into the pillow and grinded, pretending she was still there. In the wee hours of the morning my body was in the same position and I stayed in the bed much of the next day.

When I finally got out of bed, I cried. I wanted badly for Sheree to be here with me. She was right where I wanted her and I let her go.

The rest of the weekend went by much too slowly. Although I didn't have to work I rode the train into the city to get a glimpse of Sheree. When I didn't see her I spent the day in the subway station waiting for her to show up so I could apologize. She never did.

When I got home I called her numerous times. I left message after message and she never returned my calls. It was then I decided to personally deliver her flowers after work Monday. She would have to give me another chance then.

I showed up at the booth promptly at four p.m. but the station seemed deserted. Beating the after-work rush gave me time to plead my case without interruptions, and get her back in my bed tonight.

"Hi. These are for you. How are you?"

"I'm fine. Thanks. There's no room in here for the flowers so just sit them outside the door. What do you want?"

"I came to apologize and invite you over. I want to make it up to you. Please give me another chance."

Sheree looked me in my face with no emotion or expression. I could tell that she was aggravated. She would put up a fight, but I wouldn't leave until I had her.

"Tammy, I want a woman with experience. Don't get me wrong, I think you're a nice enough woman and would probably make me happy but I need more. I don't think your ready for me. I'm sorry."

"Please. Don't give up on me just yet. Give me another chance. I can make you happy in and out of the bedroom."

Seductively she asked, "Tell me what you can do then."

My body started shaking and I began to sweat. My mouth went dry and I almost couldn't speak. This girl was it for me. I had to let go of my inhibitions and show her I was it for her, too.

"Maybe you should leave. I'll call you one day."

When Sheree turned her back to me I stopped shaking and sweating. I saw myself licking her from her neck to her ass and would make it happen.

"Sheree, let me come in the booth with you. I'll show you what I can do."

She turned to face me with the same sly grin she had before. She said nothing as she opened the door. I stepped in past her and quickly squatted down, positioning myself directly in front of her on my knees. She stood still with her legs apart as I reached up and unzipped her pants. Gently I pulled them down, revealing her powder blue panties, and pressed my face into them inhaling deeply.

"Tammy, you're making me feel so good right now. I like this."

Hearing her say that made me nervous. My hands began shaking again while looking at her panties. The smell of her sweet vagina made me lose control. Instead of me being gentle and slowly tasting her I went to fast and was rough.

"Damn! I knew you were an amateur. Get up."

I didn't say anything as I tried to help Sheree pull her pants up before standing.

"I don't need your help. I know how to handle everything on my body. Get out."

As I stepped out of the booth I didn't look at her and walked to the turnstile with my head down. My posture remained that way until I arrived home.

When I walked into my place I grabbed a bottle of wine and the ice bucket. The CD player sang to me again and I fought hard to hold back tears. I then went to my bed and held the pillow tight. I had two chances with this woman and blew them both. If all I could do was pretend Sheree was here then that's what I'd do.

The usual routine of air humping and grinding came naturally. The ring of the telephone thirty minutes later brought me out of my make believe love session. Calming myself before answering didn't work.

"He, He, Hello?"

"Tammy? It's me, Sheree. What are you doing? You sound strange?"

"Oh, uh, nothing." The ice bucket stared at me as if it was humiliated. "Just ah, filling the ice bucket. Are you okay?"

"Yeah. Look, I shouldn't have treated you like that. No one has ever been nice to me like you have. Usually people just want me for pleasure so that's all I know. I guess I should say I'm sorry."

"That's okay, I understand. So, ah, do you want to come over?"

"Yeah. I kinda like you and I want to get to know you. Do you mind?"

"No, not at all. I want you here. Where are you? Do you want me to come and get you?"

"Just come open the door. I'm outside your apartment."

"I'll be right there."

The phone landed somewhere as I ran to the door faster than I did before. This time when I opened it, Sheree stood before me with a long red coat on and a pair of thigh high red boots.

She breezed past me and dropped her coat to the floor. The floor mat to the game Twister was wrapped around her body. She unwrapped it and let it fall. No other covering was on her. There was nothing that could do her justice. I closed the door.

"Take off your clothes."

Without questions, my ragged jogging pants and tee shirt came off. We faced each other naked – like a stand off, with her boots giving her more leverage than me.

"I want you to do what I say and do it well. Do you understand?"

My head shook up and down, then again, up and down, then again. I was dizzy within her.

"Go and get the ice bucket."

Sheree's voice came to me like a dominatrix in training. She spoke like she had one more test to pass before she could hold the crown. Her voice was forceful, soothing, and pleading from within for love. I listened.

When I returned to the room with the bucket as she requested she had spread the mat out, and was standing at one end of it.

"Lay the bucket in the center of the mat on the yellow circle."

I obeyed.

"Stand in the middle of the mat with my pussy over the bucket."

As I began to move I heard My, My, My from the CD. I wanted to cry out that I was in love. A figure eight, a coke bottle, her waist, her thighs, her breasts, I, I...I couldn't believe she stood before me. Her legs were spread a bit and I noticed a small tattoo high on her inner left thigh. I wanted to suck it.

"Left hand blue."

The blue circle was to my rear so I bent back and placed my hand on it.

"Right hand green."

The green circle was also to my rear. My bending more to the rear made my middle come down low over the ice bucket. I held my head back and let it hang. My body was open wide to her. She had me. Finally, I was hers.

The touch of her tongue blazed me to my heart. It pumped with anticipation. Sheree was between my legs teaching me how to love us. The ice gliding around me gave me a sensation of hot, cold, cool, and flaming at the same time. My mind ran far and came back close as she gently crawled over my body. My position was the same, my back was inner arched and my legs were open wide. She kissed my chest, my breasts, my belly button, and came back up to my neck. A tear escaped me.

"Right foot red."

I slid my foot forward not knowing where it was going to end. I didn't care; I just wanted to please Sheree.

"Left foot yellow."

This time the motion left me laying flat on my back with my eyes facing my baby. We took each other in within a twisted rhythm of euphoric colors. Her tender breasts lay on mine and my tears continued.

"Don't cry, lover."

Our lips met. I wrapped my arms around her trying to press her into me. Her hips, her ass, and her back belonged to me. I squeezed them all. My, My, My, our love came in yellow, red, blue, and green. A game so simple, yet so complex. The bucket tipped and a sensation came. More sensations followed. A game that taught me to release my fears in love. The game taught Sheree to love the one her release is with.

That night we played more than a mere child's game. We dealt our cards, we rolled our dice, and ultimately we hit the Lotto. We won them all and have never stopped pleasing each other.

We decided that night that we would work on having a relationship. Sheree thought all a relationship consisted of was sex, freaky or not. I didn't know sex was a major part of one. That was seven years ago. To this day, Sheree makes me proud to say that my rhythm is rated L.

T-Xtasy Talk

A siren attached to a speeding police vehicle rapidly approached Eva's midnight blue Mercedes Benz. She had made the purchase three days after the H-Ball, and was very cautious in her new ride. She never sped, parked away from the crowd in lots, and kept it spotless.

"Shit, I'm going three miles under the limit. What does this jerk want?"

As the police cruiser gained on her, Eva pulled over out of traffic. Instantaneously, her hand reached towards the glove compartment to get out all of her pertinent information. The sound of Sheila's voice coming from a bullhorn made her angry, made her laugh, and made her angry again—all within two seconds.

"Hey, girl, I scared you didn't I?"

Eva sighed as Sheila approached her car.

"Uh-huh…I had you going. You out here drivin' your new whip like Miss Daisy's bitch, all slow and shit."

They both burst out laughing. By this time Sheila was standing next to Eva's car. She had recently graduated from the police academy, but as a rookie, Eva thought she was still working the desk at the precinct.

"Girl, what the hell are you doing out here harassing law abiding citizens like myself?"

"Please, you broke all kinds of laws at the H-Ball!"

After the both of them cut their eyes at one another they laughed again. As they composed themselves, Sheila asked, "So Miss Big Baller, what are you doing for Thanksgiving?"

"I hadn't planned to do anything out of the ordinary. My mother is cooking and the entire family is going over there. Why? What plans do you have?"

Her eyes took on a sinister glare and she smiled before she spoke.

"Well, I just happen to have tickets to the T-Xtasy."

"The what?" Perplexed, Eva asked again. "No seriously, the what?"

"It's a huge Thanksgiving orgy party. You think a turkey has meat -you ain't seen meat like this before."

Eva laid her head back and rested her hands on her chest. After the last party she attended with Sheila, anything was possible.

"Sheila, what kind of freak are you?"

"The best kind! Gobble, gobble!"

They laughed again and Eva had to rummage through her purse to find a tissue for her eyes. Sheila placed her hand on her shoulder and massaged it gently.

"Look, I really want you to go, but don't burst a vessel – Marisol is going, too."

Eva's movements of cleaning her face stopped immediately.

"Why is it that her stank ass is always around? Damn, she really plays me close sometimes. She has been calling me, she invited me out to lunch and dinner, and she even had the nerve to ask about my personal life. I swear she acts like she's my momma."

"Or your man."

Sheila's hand flew up to cover her mouth.

"My man? What the hell does that mean?"

Placing her hands on the window crease, Sheila bent down and forward a bit.

"Uh, Eva, Marisol really likes you."

The look on Eva's face could have easily allowed her to play a victim in a horror movie.

"Hey, don't say anything. Besides, I have to get this car back to the precinct and I don't have time to listen to you scream. I'll call you tonight."

A soft squeeze was all Sheila could offer. She soothed Eva's shoulder before walking back to the cruiser. Eva glanced at her in her rearview mirror and thought aloud.

"My man? I knew something was up with her, but I never thought about that. Wow."

Sheila blew her horn as she rode past. For a second, if that, the thought of how attractive Marisol was played with her. When the second was over, Eva pulled her new ride back into traffic continuing on her way home, and shunned the advance notice of what the coming months had in store for her.

Reaching a Peak

Juleesa opened her eyes in aggravation. She squinted to look at the clock and sucked her teeth as she focused on the time.

"5:42 am. This better be good." Groggily, she reached for the receiver. "Hello?"

"Hey, Boo! You still sleepin' over there?" Mild rage engulfed her when she heard her wake up call speak.

"Pam! Why are you calling me now?"

Julessa was a definite nighthawk and on most evenings didn't turn in until the sun told her to.

"Calm down, I'll make it quick. I'm just making sure we have everything for my birthday getaway. Now, my mama is making the collard greens and fried chicken. Do you have any hot sauce? You know you can't get busy without no hot sauce!"

Idiot-filled laughter almost pushed Juleesa over the edge. Every year Pam's obsession with her birthday grew progressively worse. Sighing heavily, her eyes searched her dresser top looking for something to complete the vision of killing Pam. Her sights landed on her insulin pack.

"That would do the deed nicely."

Smacking on a helpless piece of food Pam said, "What?" A few more smacks followed. "What did you say?"

"Nothing...just thinking aloud. Yes, everything is set for your party. The only thing I have left to do is swing by the ski shop and pick up the jacket I special ordered."

"That's the red down jacket, right? The one that fits you like finger paint? Girl, Herndon is going to beg you to take him back when he sees you rocking that thing!"

Once again Pam broke out into hysterics. She didn't hear Juleesa press the end button on her cordless, or hear it crashing into the wall she hurled it at. This year Pam had begged her to plan a ski party with a group of twelve. Begrudgingly, she did and became more and more irritated, as the day grew closer. Two of the participants couldn't come up with the full amount of money, and to avoid having to pay a penalty for cancellation, she made up the difference. To make the entire ordeal even more horrific her ex fiancé, Herndon finagled his way on the trip. He heard about the three-day snow soiree from Pam's cousin, and paid her to let him be his date. Juleesa almost cancelled the entire event, but Pam cried as if she had gotten three sets of immunization shots. Alas, the trip plans forged ahead.

"Damn, Pam's old behind doesn't even like snow. She won't get on the slopes and probably won't even come out of the cabin. I know she'll have on a bleach blonde wig with matted hair going down her back and gold lip-gloss. Oh, I wish I could just disappear."

The jarring sound of her doorbell blared suddenly, which drew her out of her Pam rant, but sent her into another wicked mood.

"What in the hell is going on this morning? Geesh…"

Juleesa angrily thrust her body out of bed. She stumbled a bit as her feet hit the floor and cursed whoever it was at the door.

"If you're not bleeding and dead you're ass is going to wish you were!"

Those were the only words she said before she swung the door open to see Herndon.

"What do you want?"

Her voice was short and filled with resentment. The man that stood before her had once been her only love. There was a time when she wanted to give him babies and a love that would last always. Juleesa hated the fact that she still wanted him. Not caring to view all of him she cut her eyes to a slit. Her breathing was heavy and deep and made her breasts move up and down seductively. She didn't bother to put on her robe and stood before him wearing a sheer lace pink teddy. His eyes took in her anger before he spoke.

"I'm sorry to wake you so early. I couldn't sleep, J. I had to see you."

Juleesa stared at Herndon and his passion filled gaze. She knew he'd made a mistake and didn't care if he spent the rest of his life trying to get her back.

Her anger never stayed long when Herndon was involved. Sighing was an admission of defeat to her longing feelings. She stepped back from the doorframe and moved over to invite him inside.

"Do you want some coffee? Juice?"

Smiling he said, "No, I'm fine." He walked towards the couch where they once made love nightly. When he was seated, he patted the cushion next to him. She felt if she sat so close, he'd have his way, so she went and sat in his favorite recliner.

Her nipples began to harden and the wetness between her thighs caused her to squirm lightly in place. She squeezed her muscles in an attempt to cease the moisture but her efforts were to no avail. Knowing she'd always be defeated by her emotions for Herndon she relaxed, and awaited his reason for being there.

"I know I'm the last person you want to talk to but I have to get this off of my chest. I want this weekend to be relaxing for us. I want to spend time with you. I'm here so you can cuss me out, beat me down, or do whatever you feel in your heart before we get there."

She grew angry again. Lately, whenever she spoke with Herndon she couldn't help but think he was always out for himself. The fact that she was half asleep escalated her mood and made this time no different.

"You came here this early to say that? Why? Do you have some trick that's coming along? You need to make a good impression? You don't want the ex anchor making you look like the Bull Mastiff you are?"

Through her anger, Juleesa didn't realize that as she leaned forward her legs spread wide. One of her breasts had risen up during her tirade to Herndon and was showing itself full on. She could feel his vapors as he enjoyed the view of her delicious sexual passage, and her sweet nipple. She made Herndon begin to peak and he hadn't even touched her yet.

"Why are you staring at me like that?"

Her breath was bursting out of her. It surged hot with lust. She perspired a scent that pulled Herndon to her. The same scent drowned her senses and made her see him as the man she wanted to have her. Her mind's haze took her into another world and she didn't realize how much of her body was exposed.

Herndon stood, walked over to her and then knelt between her legs. He placed his hands on her thighs and slid them up and down slowly in an exotic rhythm. His touch calmed her instantly. She sat back in the chair, making her legs open wider. She raised her hands to her chest and wasn't startled by the fact that she felt her skin instead of lace.

Pressing his lips into her flesh Herndon inhaled her fragrance. It was always engaging and natural, and he slid his tongue around her leg to show his pleasure.

"Oh, J, you are divine. Let me come home, please?"

Juleesa closed her eyes and allowed her thoughts to marvel at the idea of being with him once again. She and Herndon had met when the both of them had graduated High School. They went on to college together and were inseparable. Herndon was the only man she'd ever been with. He left her standing at the alter because he said he suddenly got cold feet. She could no longer see herself smiling. Reliving the feelings from that day pushed the picture of a happy reunion out of her mind.

"Stop it, Herndon. This is wrong. I can't do this."

Juleesa pushed his head away and regrouped. She returned her body back to its composed state and stepped over the hunching broken man in her living room.

"I'd appreciate it if you leave now."

Noticing her stern voice Herndon did nothing to object to her. He stood slowly and walked to the door without facing her. Before he stepped outside he stopped.

"I know you hate me but I love you. I made a mistake. Forgive me."

He then walked away without looking back. After they split up he moved five blocks over from her. Juleesa watched him walk down the sidewalk and began to cry. She loved him and wanted them to marry. If she could only get the phantom that kept telling her he'd stand her up again out of her ear, maybe that would happen.

The sleep she awakened from that morning would have to wait until that night to join her. The thought of the last time they made love swept over her. She went and lay on the couch, in the spot that Herndon had just vacated, and closed her eyes. She felt his strong hands undressing her and caressing her body. He roamed her like a cellist stroked their strings, effortlessly and with precision. Each time he kissed her nude body she'd moan a tune they orchestrated. The sound of the phone once again took her peacefulness away.

"Oh, this day is unbearable!"

She reached for the phone and noticed the number on the ID box.

"What Pam? What is it now?"

"Boo, I'm going to pick you up, okay? Delia was going to drive us but she's going to ride with Herndon and Guy. I'll be there at three."

Screaming Juleesa slammed the phone down.

"Oh! I hate him! I knew they had something going on! He's going to pay for this!"

The rest of the day she stomped around. She ran her errands and packed her bag for the trip, all the while planning to ruin Herndon's weekend. In her mind she saw Delia trying to throw the fact in her face that her ex and she were an item. She paced around for a few minutes fighting back tears that came from the loss of her pending marriage. When she could no longer conceal her feelings she spoke out loud to the only person that would listen.

"God, please let the next three days pass without me acting a fool. You know I love Herndon and I want to be his wife. But I'm so afraid that he is going to hurt me. What should I do? Please give me a sign."

Juleesa sighed and fell to the floor. Her tears fell until Pam honked her horn, signaling the beginning of the dreaded ski trip.

When Pam saw Juleesa walking to the car she hopped out and ran up the walk to greet her. She opened her arms wide and swooped her in them like she was a giddy two-year old.

"Okay, Pam... I'm happy to see you, too," was all Juleesa could squeeze out through her crushed body. Pam continued to compact her and slung her from side to side.

"I'm just happy that you planned this!"

Pam screamed this directly into her ear. Usually, Juleesa would dig into her, but since it was her birthday she let it slide.

When they finally separated they loaded up the car. Pam turned up the volume on the CD that played and it actually put Juleesa in the mood for partying and skiing. R. Kelly's song, Feelin' On Yo Booty, came on and her thoughts instantly raced to Herndon. He never stayed far from her mind and she secretly fantasized about being with him at the lodge.

After riding for three hours up to a remote mountain region in Upstate New York, they arrived at the Snow Blade Ski Resort. Juleesa and Pam were the sixth and seventh members of their group to get there. Three of Pam's co-workers and two of her cousins had come up the night before. Since Juleesa had made the arrangements previously all they had to do was check in, receive their slope passes, and get their tickets for the free breakfast buffet and drink specials.

Herndon pulled into the parking lot just as Juleesa was removing her last bag from the trunk. His passengers included Delia, who happened to be seated in the front next to him, and the three remaining guests. She couldn't help but get annoyed upon seeing another woman riding in the seat she used to occupy. Instead of her being the gracious host she threw her bag over her shoulder, slammed the trunk down and trudged off into the lodge.

That night Pam's party entourage turned in early. The group had a six a.m. wake up call for the first lift up the mountain and everyone wanted to be well rested.

In the breakfast line the next morning Juleesa avoided making eye contact with Herndon. When she saw him approaching the ladies table she excused herself and went to the restroom. It was time to leave when she came back out and she hurried outside to join the group. While waiting on the shuttle to pick them up he made his way over to her.

"Good morning, J. Hey, uh, if it's cool with you maybe we can sneak off somewhere later on and talk."

She turned to him. She desperately wanted to kiss him but held her feelings at bay. She cut her eyes at Delia before she spoke.

"That's the problem with you. You always want to sneak."

Before he could respond the van pulled up and she quickly took a seat. The ride up to the mountain was spent with them two staring at each other and listening to instructions from the guide. Since most of them were intermediate skiers they were to be paired off into groups. They were instructed how to turn their feet to avoid collisions and the best way to get up if they fell. Two of the members were given radios in case of an emergency. With that, the ride was complete. Everyone excited the shuttle eager to slide down Lover's Peak, the highest slope at the resort.

Once they were suited up a lifeline was connected to hooks on their waistbands. Pam was at the head of her group. She stood at the top of the peak and bent her knees as if she was a professional. Right before she went over the edge she yelled,

"Happy Birthday to me!" and down she went. That was the only time Juleesa had laughed since arriving. Herndon noticed it and took that opportunity to get on her good side. He waved. She instantly stopped chuckling and moved up closer to the top of the slope. Her group was next and concentrating on him would have to wait. Delia and Herndon were behind her and she couldn't wait to kick up snow in their faces.

Suddenly, the snow beneath her began sliding and she heard a loud rumbling roar.

"A-V-A-L-A-N-C-H-E!"

Snow. Ice. Cold. Pain. Tumbling, rolling, spiraling downward without control. Flipping, turning, twisting unable to grasp onto anything grounded, Juleesa's mind rolled the same as her body.

"I keep on falling, and falling and falling. Alicia Keys shut up. Oh, God, help me. I'm going to die."

So many thoughts hurried into her mind.

"My backpack. Shit, there goes my backpack. My medicine, my candy. Not only am I going to die, I'm going to go into a diabetic fit before I gasp my last breath. Damn my body aches. My legs, my ass and even my breasts are throbbing with pain."

The crunching sound of hard snow smacking her in the face bought tears to her eyes.

"Snow, I hate snow. Why did I agree to plan this stupid trip?"

Her mind played a game of chance as she continued plummeting.

"Why was I so mean to Herndon? He's probably screwing Delia right now. His sorry ass should be buried somewhere underneath all of this snow. Maybe we'll have to munch on him for survival."

As soon as her last thought lingered in her mind she immediately stopped.

"Juleesa! Juleesa can you hear me? Juleesa! Where are you?"

"His ass ain't buried? This is a bad day."

Juleesa's body pained all over but she managed to yell, "Herndon, I'm okay! I'm over here somewhere."

"Don't move. I'll come to you."

Just then a light tug pulled at her back. It grew stronger as he got closer. They were divorced in life but still connected by a buddy cable.

Juleesa sucked her teeth as she muttered, "Damn buddy cable."

Two massive hands covered with black gloves reached through the snow mound on top of her. Slowly and carefully, they worked painstakingly to pull her out. She was beaten and bruised, but still breathing.

"Hey you...how ya feeling?"

Juleesa's heart melted when she saw his face.

"Considering the circumstances I'm okay. How about you?"

"A little sore but I'll live. I wonder how everyone else is. We can rest up for a bit and then head back down to look for them."

"As much as I've rolled aren't we back at the bottom?"

"No. We only fell about thirty-feet. I guess it seemed like more with all the snow."

"Why in the world did Darin yell avalanche then?"

"I don't know; this is a manmade mountain. And besides, you know Darin is dramatic."

Herndon waved his arms around and pouted his lips. That's exactly how Darin would look if he were with them. Usually his antics brought a smile to her face. She stifled it this time, though.

"I have to get out of here now. Damn. When is this day going to be over?"

"Relax, J. I'll take care of you."

Her eyes rolled hard three times before she said, "Where is everybody else at?"

"Probably scattered about. You and I were connected along with Lorne and Delia. Before we fell Lorne unhooked us so the two of them could be alone. I'm sure they're all fine. Like I said, I'll take care of you."

"Lorne and Delia have something going on?"

Juleesa was happy that she had been wrong about her.

"J, I told you I only want you. Trust me."

Herndon actually looked good with snow as an accessory. Some of it was stuck to his beard and Juleesa suddenly wanted to lick it off. She quickly shook that vision from her mind. Despite the cold conditions and her desire to have him as her husband again, her attitude was hot and nasty.

"I don't see how that's possible. You couldn't do it when we were together."

With the only logical answer he could give he responded.

"Do you see anybody else around here that can help you?"

Bitter words came from her mouth.

"Hell no. I can't believe I agreed to this."

"Pam is adventurous. Besides, this is a good place for couples to spend time together."

"If the male isn't a pussy hound I'm sure this would be a nice place."

She narrowed her eyes to a near close and stared at him hard. Who was he to comment on a couple? Before she could blast him a new hole as to how he ruined her life, he sensed her feelings, and spoke before she could voice them.

"Regardless of the past we're all we have right now. Can we at least agree to work together until we get out of here?"

Juleesa was weak and on the verge of fainting but could still muster up enough strength to slap the shit out of him. Instead, she agreed to his terms.

"Fine. What shall we do?"

"First, we should huddle close, as to keep warm, and then work our way back down the mountain. The cable is buried but we'll be able to use it as a guide."

Concerned she asked, "Huddle close?"

"Look, J. It's a survival tactic. Body heat is the only thing we have right now."

"I don't feel so well."

Pleading he said, "I won't try anything. I promise."

"No, it's not that. I lost my backpack with my insulin and my chocolate."

Herndon pulled her close and began rubbing his hands feverously around her body. She chilled first, and then began to warm and react to his touch.

"Is this better?"

"Yes. It's helping. I'll be okay. I'm nervous and fighting off a panic attack."

"I have some power bars in my jacket. Will one of those help?"

"I'll eat it later if I need to. Thanks."

Neither of them spoke for the next few minutes. Herndon continued to warm her with his hands. He slid them underneath her jacket and Juleesa gave in. Although they were in an awkward situation, she thought of rolling in the snow, consumed in ecstasy with him. As if they were in their old bedroom, she reached her arms up and wrapped them around Herndon's neck. On cue, their lips and tongues met, and shuffled within each other's mouths like they were home.

"Damn I've missed you, J."

With that, bomber jackets, scarves, and warm padding were removed.

Suddenly nervous she asked, "What if somebody sees us?"

"Then it will be their best avalanche ever."

She forgot about it being cold, the snow and the fact that her body hurt all over. Juleesa even forgot that she couldn't stand Herndon; she just loved him. They pulled away from each other and she threw her jacket on a low mound. Then, she lay down in a snow angel position, waiting for what he had. He bent slightly and pulled her snow pants, her long silk underwear, and her panties down around her knees. Warm hands then lifted and spread her legs, and a sexy, large, semi sweet dark frame slid in between them.

"Ahhh, I'm finally home."

"Give me all the chocolate I'll ever need."

In one quick movement, Herndon whipped out the one thing that always gave her a lift. It was delicately warm, and he glided him into her with smooth precision, and began a slow hump that escalated into long, fast strokes. They pumped, bumped, caressed, sucked, and rolled until their passion began to melt the chill between them. His weight pressed her body further into the snow, which gave her the tingling sensation of coldness along with heat on her backside. She loved the feeling.

Herndon's breathing quickened and he yelled, "Ohh, Juleesa!"

Her body shivered and jerked as she met his hot thick liquid with her own. Their bodies bucked in unison for a few minutes, and then lay still, paying no attention to their wilderness surroundings.

Herndon exhaled.

"Baby, that was excellent. I miss you, J."

Juleesa wanted to tell him the same but decided to make him work to make her his wife. And she would be his wife. He didn't love anyone but her. As soon as they returned to civilization, she'd take him back. He is the man she loved.

"Let's talk about that when we get home. Come' on, lead me out of here."

They returned to their upright positions and looked once again like two people who had been snowbound. As they made it back down the mountain hand in hand to the place that saved Juleesa's soul, she thought of all the memories she and Herndon would make. Her inside smile radiated as she visualized them on a thick rug in her cabin, creating their very own romantic movie that she'd title reaching a peak.

Room With A View

"Oh, I hate being stuck in traffic. I'm already twenty minutes late as it is. I hope the realtor is still there. This house has got to be the perfect one. I've been looking for one for over two months now and haven't found anything suitable. They either have too much room, not enough room, or are just plain dumps. And the asking prices are ridiculous."

Having less than ten minutes before she'd be considered late, Bertice continued to maneuver through the rush hour traffic. Her mind wandered to times past as she talked to her invisible riding partner.

"I never thought I'd have to move again this late in life, but George's passing makes staying in our home unbearable. You'd think I'd want to be there where all of our memories are but I can't. I just pray that I'm able to adjust better than I've been doing. Throwing away our bed seemed like the right thing to do at the time, but now I miss it dearly. Well, I'm not going to dwell on that right now. I have one more turn to make and hopefully I'll be at my new place."

Bertice slowed her blue Lexus down to a near standstill. Her heart skipped a few beats as she took in the splendor of the home that stood before her. It was a split-level ranch that had the comfort and beauty of a quaint cottage. This had to be the one; her search had to be over. She slowly exited her car as her realtor, Mr. Marvin, approached her.

"Mrs. Harvey. Welcome. I'm so glad you made it. I know the traffic was heavy today so I expected you to be a little late. How are you?"

"I'm fine, Mr. Marvin. Thank you. I'm sorry I'm late. I decided at the last minute to keep our appointment and left the office without calling. Please forgive me."

"Apology accepted. Let's get started. As I told you earlier I think this is the perfect place for you. It has all the amenities you requested and the price is well within your range. Shall we take a look inside?"

"Yes, I'd love to. I love the way it looks on the outside. Let's hope the inside makes me feel the same way."

Inhaling and a small prayer escaped Bertice before she stepped inside Sixty-Three Forty-Four Hunter Drive. She closed and opened her eyes as she exhaled and smiled. This was it. This was the home where she'd try to begin her life over again.

"So, Mrs. Harvey, do you like it? Or should I just take the smile on your face as a yes?"

Bertice giggled before responding. She hadn't felt this good about anything since before her husband's passing. One good feeling was the only sign she needed to make her decision.

"Mr. Marvin, this home is beautiful. I feel as if it's giving me a hug. I don't care what the cost is; I'll take it."

"Whew, thank goodness. I didn't know what I'd do if you didn't like this one."

Hearty laughs immediately followed his comment. She had been a little pushy and difficult in her search, but he never commented or complained. He knew what her reasons were and did his best to help her.

"I'm sorry for being such a pain to you, Mr. Marvin. I guess I was a little diva-like sometimes. I'll tell you what; the first dinner prepared in my new home will be for you. How about it?"

"You have yourself a deal, Mrs. Harvey. Let's take a look at the upstairs. I think you'll find all the rooms match your descriptions perfectly."

"I'm sure they will. All I've really wanted is a nice sized room to write in - my own personal space where I can let my words flow. Someplace where I can see my visions and make them come to life - my own room with a view."

"Then this is definitely the place for you."

Bertice followed Mr. Marvin up the stairs with a light gait. She wanted to sign the papers right then. The house had been vacant for some time now and Mr. Marvin told her she could move in ASAP. After seeing the entire home that was fine with her. It was perfect. She planned to begin her move the upcoming weekend.

"Do you have anymore questions before we leave, Mrs. Harvey"?

"No, not at this point. Well, maybe one. I know this to be a good area, but what about my next-door neighbors? Do you know anything about them?"

An informative scholar took over Mr. Marvin's body.

"Sure. The house on your left belongs to an elderly couple named Hill. They've lived there since the 1960's and have no children. They have a couple of dogs, but I'm sure they'll be no problem."

"Sounds good. And on my right?"

The scholar paced while he continued sharing his knowledge.

"A young man named David Greer. I've met him twice when I showed the house before. I believe he works in the city and attends night school. He seemed like a very respectable young man when we met. Maybe you can get him to be your handy man."

"When I introduce myself I'll ask. Now let's go and get started on my closing papers. I have a move to make."

Bertice took the next three weeks off from work. She'd been employed with the Reliable Insurance Company since she was twenty-two and had more than enough vacation and personal days. The company had always been good to her and gave her promotions regularly. She was the head of the underwriting department and could handle many of her duties from home. Her boss, Mrs. Parker, was more than happy to give her the time off. They all had a hard time dealing with the death of Bertice's husband and looked forward to the day when she'd be happy again.

The movers arrived early on Saturday morning and finished before three p.m. Bertice had only kept the necessities and some of her husband's personal belongings. She was in no rush to get the entire home organized, but did want to get her workroom done. She had the layout planned perfectly in her mind for months and couldn't wait to make it a reality. All she really needed to do was hang a few pictures, place her desk and chair in the correct position, and put her knick-knacks and such where they belonged.

When Bertice finally had her room set up she decided to take a nice long bubble bath and then settle into a productive night of writing. Her love had always been that of becoming a published writer and wanted dearly to accomplish it before her husband passed.

Before going in to bathe Bertice sat in her chair and thought of their life together. She reflected on the year they were married as she gazed out her window and unknowingly into her neighbor's window. The blinds were raised and she quickly jumped up to close them when she realized what she was looking at. She blushed and felt embarrassed as she peeked between them into her neighbor David's bedroom and watched him undress.

"Oh my goodness," Bertice mumbled. "Oh my goodness."

Her husband, George, had been gone for over two years. Bertice had never been with, or let alone, thought of another man. The most excitement she'd received since her husband's death was the pleasure of her monthly douche routine. The long nozzle worked wonders on lonely evenings while Bertice thought of nights gone by with George. Although she was a one time beauty pageant queen, and could still give any young contestant a run for their money, she felt that part of her life left with her husband. She felt ashamed continuing to stare at David this way but she couldn't help it. She ran and turned off the light as not to get caught, and returned to her window, peeking out like a naughty little schoolgirl who knew she was doing wrong.

Sitting down clamed her a bit as she spoke her thoughts out loud while watching David. Her body grew hot and she occasionally wiggled in her seat.

"My, my, my how things have changed. I didn't know a man could look so good. Oh, Bertice, you should be ashamed of yourself. This boy could be your son. But he's not. Oooh, he's taking off his underwear. Oh my goodness."

Placing her hand over her mouth Bertice began touching herself. David was totally nude at that point and she wanted him in her bed.

"George, forgive me."

Her eyes wouldn't allow her to stop staring as David turned to walk out of the room, and most likely into his bathroom.

"Uhm, uhm, uhm. Look at the behind on him. I think I'll make an introduction tonight. Wait a minute, what am I saying? I'm a married woman. I can't do this. I shouldn't have these kinds of thoughts about someone else's child. I need to take a cold shower and get David out of my mind."

Bertice went into the bathroom and stuck with the plan of the bubble bath. While in the tub she laid back and closed her eyes. Usually she saw herself with George, but this time David's face and body filled her mind. As she fingered herself she saw him touching her breasts and kissing her body all over. David was quite handsome and had all the right tools to go with it. A good guess would put him at about six-feet-four inches with a muscular build. She was sure he worked out. He was clean-shaven with a hot bronze complexion that she wanted to touch.

"Somebody help me. I shouldn't have thoughts like this. I have to meet him. Tonight, I'll make that young man mine. Oh, God, help me."

Hopping out of the tub and oiling her body down was her first move. Her skin had always been baby soft smooth and sweet. She was very health conscience and could easily pass for a fine woman in her late thirty's. Her body was firm with robust breasts and wide hips. Her slender well-toned legs kept the men looking and making catcalls for years. She could see David's bronze mixing with her mocha to create a beautiful color.

Bertice threw on a red sundress with low-heeled sandals and made it as far as her front door. All her talk would be cheap tonight, and for the next two weeks. Although she saw herself with David and wanted it to happen, she couldn't get up the nerve. She was content with watching him from the window every morning and every night. When she began setting her alarm clock as not to miss him, she changed her mind.

"Okay, Bertice. Tonight is the night. I'll bake a nice cake and take it over as a neighborly, friendship offering. I've never seen any visitors come by, so it could be possible that he's single."

Bertice syked herself up more by having a few glasses of port sherry. She was well relaxed after watching David undress. Just as she stepped out the door a car pulled up in front of David's house. Quickly, she stepped back in and closed the door. She sat the cake down on the floor and leaned against the door momentarily. Then she opened it slightly and looked through the crack.

She saw David strolling down the sidewalk to meet a very attractive young woman. David walked around to the woman's door and helped her out of the car. The two of then kissed lovingly on the lips, held hands, and walked back inside his home.

Bertice used the door to slide down on the floor, pushing the cake over with her feet. She felt like an elderly woman then and was glad she didn't get the chance to embarrass herself. She sat there for about a half an hour before she decided to go write her feelings down. If she couldn't have David for real she could put him in her book pages. There he could be close to her always.

Slowly, Bertice walked up the stairs and sluggishly into her room. She didn't bother to turn the light on and went straight to her chair. She didn't plan on spying on David tonight but couldn't take her eyes away from the window.

She sat up and felt excited when she saw David and his guest enter his room with lighted candles. They placed them in various places and met in the middle. They pulled close and kissed as they undressed each other. Bertice began to unbutton her top and touch her breasts when she saw what was going on.

David then took his guest by the hand and led her to his bed. They sat down side-by-side and continued getting undressed. The woman then lie back and David got on top of her.

Bertice stood up and took all her clothes off. She pressed her body up against the blinds and grinded slowly.

"Oh my goodness. What are you doing? Get away from the window now."

She continued to grind and entered herself with three fingers. She squatted a bit and moved them in and out of her slowly as she watched David's movements.

"That young man knows what he's doing. I don't care what kind of company he has; I'm going to meet him."

Bertice watched David for much of the night. When she realized they'd gone to sleep she went to her bedroom and did the same. She'd decided that tomorrow night would be her turn and nothing would make her change her mind.

The next day at work everyone noticed how Bertice glowed and floated around the office. Mrs. Parker had to know what was the cause of this and pulled Bertice into her office for the four-one-one.

"I notice a big difference in you today. I'm very happy to see it, but I really want to know the cause of it. Care to share your secret?"

"Nothing much, Laverne. My new home has come together very well and I'm just happy."

"You sure that's all it is? There's not another someone special these days? I know you spent a lot of time with your realtor. Could he be the reason for your new attitude?"

Bertice gave a hush your mouth grin. She couldn't dare tell what was really going on. They'd been friends since she began the job and told each other everything. Laverne had to be left with something juicy.

"Oh, Laverne. I won't tell you a thing now, but keep your fingers crossed. I may have news of an upcoming sexual encounter real soon."

Walking away without another word Laverne stood with her hands over her mouth. She badly hoped she'd have some news to tell soon and wanted David to be the reason for it.

Bertice didn't get a chance to meet David until three weeks later. He always left very early and came home late. The day she came home from work and saw his car was when she planned to go over and get her treat. She went upstairs and looked in his window. She saw him leaving his room and ran downstairs quickly to grab the pie she bought and make her introduction.

She timed it perfectly and knocked on his door just as he walked downstairs. She squeezed her vagina muscles when she heard him opening the door.

He's gorgeous. "Hello neighbor. I live next door. My name is Bertice. How are you?"

She felt herself beginning to sweat. She never approached a man and really didn't know what to do or say. Suddenly, she felt like an old lonely fool and wanted to run back home.

"Hello, Bertice. My name is David. I must apologize for not introducing myself sooner. It's just that when you're home I'm usually gone and vice versa. This is the first night I've had off in weeks."

" I'm sorry for intruding. You must want some time alone. Here, I'll leave you with this and come back another time."

Her mind prayed that David would ask her to come in. Walking away would make her feel unneeded.

"No, no. I should've had you over long before now. And you bought a pie, too? Please, come in."

David stepped aside and held the door open for Bertice. She walked in slowly and slightly touched his abdomen with her arm. Her skin tingled and she received the first orgasm from a man besides her husband.

"Here, let me take that. Have a seat on the sofa. I'll put this in the kitchen and get us something to drink. Do you want anything in particular?"

"Anything you bring is fine with me. I'm not picky."

"I was going to indulge in some red wine. Would you like some of that?"

"That'll be fine."

Her only thought as she glanced around David's home was that it was very well kept for a single man. He had various pieces of artwork placed throughout the room that looked to be expensive. She stood up to admire a picture over his fireplace and noticed a large decorated coffee cup. The cup held a supply of condoms. Having never used one before, she reached inside to examine them. She smiled as she read the labels saying flavored, colored and the tickler. David reentering the room clearing his throat startled her, and turned her face a hot red hue.

"Uhm, I'm sorry. I didn't mean to disturb you. You're not embarrassed are you?"

"Oh, uh, well, a little. I've never used a condom before."

David's silence was the signal for Bertice to elaborate.

"Let me explain. I'm a widower. I was married for thirty-five years and have only been with my husband. There was never any need to use a condom. I shouldn't have been so nosey and gone through your things anyway. Are you going to ask me to leave now?"

"Me, kick a beautiful woman like you out? Never. Come. Sit with me so we can get acquainted."

David held out his hand and Bertice took it. It was strong and gentle at the same time. The shame and embarrassment she felt for looking at him were no longer there when they touched. They sat comfortably side by side on the sofa and began a conversation that lasted half the night.

"So, Bertice. It seems we know all there is to know about one another. How would you like a tour of my place?"

I thought you'd never ask. "I'd love a tour. Your home is very different from mine. Lead the way."

David helped Bertice off the sofa. They'd finished two bottles of wine and she was a little wobbly. She tried to hide it but stumbled instead.

"Are you okay? I hope I didn't give you too much to drink."

"Tsk, don't be silly, David. I'm a grown woman. I can handle myself."

His eyes met hers softly.

"A grown beautiful woman at that. I hope I'm not being too forward by saying that. I don't want you to feel uncomfortable."

The wine made her a wonder woman without fear.

"David, I have a confession to make. Maybe I better show you instead. Take me to your bedroom."

He didn't say a word as he led Bertice up the stairs to his room. He turned the light on as they stepped inside and turned to face her.

"I've been watching you daily from my place through that window. The first time I did it was by accident. Then I kept doing it. I watched you make love to another woman. That's one of the reasons I came over. I had the silly notion that you'd want to make love to me. I think I'd better leave now. I'm sorry."

"Leave? Why? Why wouldn't I want you? You're a very desirable woman. Any man would want you."

"David, I'm fifty-nine. I'm old enough to be your grandmother."

"I'm thirty-three. I'm old enough to make love to you. Now tell me which one you'd like? Flavored, colored or the tickler?"

"Ahh, I don't know about this. I haven't been with a man in two years. I think I made a mistake in coming here."

"Come closer. Let me refresh your memory."

David pulled Bertice close to him and placed his lips on hers. She melted in his arms as they kissed.

"Tell me, beautiful. What flavor?"

"The tickler."

David picked her up and placed her on his bed. He then straddled her gently and began undressing her. Bertice turned her head momentarily to look out the window. She smiled inside when she saw herself looking at her and David. After undressing himself he spread her legs slightly. Then he reached in the nightstand by his bed and pulled out the tickler.

He then slid the condom on as Bertice watched without blinking.

He entered her slowly and began a melodic rhythm. Bertice tensed up for a moment but relaxed soon after. She wrapped her arms tightly around his back and her legs around his waist.

"Oh my goodness. This is wonderful."

"Just hold on, baby. Just hold on."

David moved faster and kissed her all over her face and neck. He massaged her breasts and made Bertice release constantly.

"Oh, my. Oh, my. Oh, George. Oh, George." Bertice froze after calling George's name. She returned to her rhythm after David soothed her.

"Don't worry, beautiful. It's okay. You feel good. Oooooh, you're making me work. Uh, this is good."

Raising her body slightly off the bed she began thrusting her hips hard. She was always a little timid in the bedroom. This time she wanted to make sure she'd get a return visit.

"Bertice…"

David held Bertice tightly as he filled the tickler up. Afterwards, he laid his body on hers and continued kissing her face.

"David, thank you. You don't know how good you've made me feel."

"You made me feel good as well. I've never had an older women tell me that she was attracted to me. Knowing you watch me through the window is a turn on. Will you spend the night?"

"Oh, no, David. I think I need to take this one-step at a time. Can I visit you again?"

"I understand. You can visit me anytime you like."

They kissed seductively and helped each other get dressed. He then walked her to her door and kissed her before she went in. Bertice walked up the stairs glowing like she hadn't done in the last two years. She went into her room and sat in the chair. Although the vision she had became a reality she still loved to look from her room with a view.

SHE

THE STORY OF TASHA AND JAVAR

Javar stroked his long, hard, erection fast and furious during his fifth bathroom break. All morning his dick teased him of the events of last night, and he could no longer hide, nor handle himself in the office. It was only eleven a.m., and although he managed to make his erection subside the four previous times, his control had waned. The desire of needing a magnificent release overpowered him.

The men's bathroom was empty and the thought of discharging his cum into a urinal was exciting, but risky. Not wanting to lose his job, Javar positioned himself in the last stall directly in front of the toilet, and jacked himself to his freaky content.

"Uhmmm, oh shit...ahh, here it cums...shit."

Just as Javar was about to receive his pleasure, the door opened, and he heard his co-worker, Nate, call his name.

"J-Money? Man, you in here? I need help with Excel on my computer. You know that shit always confuses me."

Muttering was all he could do.

"Damn, Nate has the worst timing in the world."

Javar managed to mute his orgasmic yell, and instead, panted heavily as his hot fluid filled the inside of the bowl. Becoming lost in his moment, Javar spoke aloud.

"Boy that felt good."

Inquisitively Nate asked, "Man, you say something?"

Sweat beaded Javar's entire forehead and lip brow. Not wanting to look suspicious, he quickly grabbed tissue, wiped his face, and threw it into the flushed bowl with the rest of the evidence.

"I'll be out in a minute."

Looking at his dick and muffling a thank you, he pulled up his pants and emerged with a beaming smile on his face.

"J, yo ass been in here five times today. Is ya dick burning?"

Nate was nosey as all hell. He was damn near gay, and watched all the men as if they were his brown-bagged lunch walking away.

"Hell naw, man. I just had a few too many beers last night. They fukin' with me now. I'll be right out."

"Aight."

When Nate exited the men's room, Javar turned his attentions to the wall mirror in front of him. The smile he had returned when he thought about being with his lady last night. The electricity She made surge through his body when they were together was undeniably sexy. It was her way of seducing him every time he caressed, or ran his hands around her smooth, sleek frame. The vision of the two of them together made him want to pleasure himself again.

She was perfect in every way imaginable. She never complained about how much time Javar spent with her and was pleased whenever he turned her on. She would do everything in her power to satisfy him, opening his mind to new and exciting adventures. She introduced him to an entire world he knew nothing of. She was becoming the very being of his imagination. She made his every desire a reality, bringing his fantasies to light. She was what he'd longed for.

As Javar made his way from the men's room to Nate's workstation, annoying beeps of the phone on his desk interrupted the thoughts of his lust filled evening. Glancing at the wall clock and assuming it was Tasha calling to nag about lunch plans, he trotted over to answer it.

"Hey, Tasha. What's up?"

"You know what's up. What time are you picking me up? It's almost twelve, and the breakfast I had wore off at ten. I'm starved."

Tasha's speaking in her wimpy way irritated the fuck out of Javar. She made last night wonderful until he heard her voice. The whine was spine numbing, and bowing to her every demand was the only way he could silence it.

"I'll be there at 12:15. I have to take a look at Nate's computer and then I'll leave."

Never, ever satisfied she continued.

"Fuck his sweet ass! Can't you leave now, baby? After last night, I really need to see you."

"I should have never told you that shit about Nate. Look, I said 12:15. I'll see you soon."

Clearly aggravated Javar slammed the phone down. Nate turned his way and gave him a heads up. Silently mumbling, "You're not my type," caused Javar to grin. His mind then returned to the perfect sexual release he had. How could he make Tasha understand that being needy only made matters worse?

Rebooting the computer solved the Excel glitch problem. Nate tried to make small talk in the process, but he was nauseating. That shit wasn't for him. He would never need a substitute for his Charmin. Soon they would all understand that his world was complete. She was all he needed.

Not wanting to be late, Javar grabbed his cell phone, jacket, and keys off of his desk, and made his way to the elevator. His office was on the tenth floor, and usually his rides down to the lobby at lunchtime were lonely. Most of the people on his floor ate lunch in the cafeteria down the hall, but today, Javar needed his elevator ride to be in silence.

Upon stepping into the elevator, She filled his mind once again. When the doors closed, She summoned him to massage his dick, and simulate his hips as if She were there. As he descended, Javar moaned out loud to the images She displayed for him. She made him feel wonderful and uninhibited. Noticing the camera viewing his every movement, Javar turned his back and moved into the corner. He couldn't stop his erection from growing to it's normal eight inches, and pumped the air between his obsession ravaged body and the corner until he filled his boxer briefs, and slacks, with more of what She wanted.

"Shit...I have to get a grip. What am I gonna do now?" Leaning forward his head rested against the wall. He was still excited, but the chime of the bell signaling his exit and the door opening saved him from another command performance.

Thinking of an encore with his favorite lady that evening gave Javar another rise for all to see. Vicki, the front desk receptionist smirked and frowned her face as he walked passed. It was obvious she'd seen his humping activity in the elevator and wasn't pleased. Still, he gave her a smile. She was the only one who mattered.

Hopping into his Infinity and turning on the radio drifted his mind away from his sticky pants. Inhaling the smell of what She brought out of him, and listening to Computer Love was his noontime erotica.

The woman standing outside of her office building pouting while looking at her watch subsided his fantasy quick. No matter what She did, Tasha had a way of ruining everything. Javar knew She needed all of his attention. The fact that Tasha didn't want to understand was the cause of so much stress in their relationship.

Slowing his car to a stop he got out to open the passenger door. As he reached for the handle, Tasha grabbed his hand and swung him around to face her.

"Baby, never mind the door. Give me a kiss."

Hesitating, he asked, "I thought you were starving. We can kiss later. Besides, everyone is looking."

Not one to take rejection easily, Tasha pulled him closer and ignored his words. She pressed her lips against his, her breasts against his chest, and slid her hands down to his crotch area. Feeling the wetness between his legs was the reason for her abrupt stop.

"Fuck, Javar! What the hell have you been doing?"

Still not embarrassed about what he'd done, he pulled away from her and walked around to the driver's side. He opened his door, sat back in his car, and waited for her to do the same. When Tasha didn't move, Javar powered her window down and asked if they were still going to lunch.

"I said I was starved didn't I?" Swinging the door open and then slamming it in frustration she added, "What is your problem lately? I can't figure you out. I give you everything you want and it's not enough. I want us to get counseling."

Annoyed he answered, "I'm not doing that. I'm fine. I've had a lot of things on my mind. You don't seem to understand."

Pulling off he noticed Tasha viewing him from the corner of his eye. Sensing an argument was coming he turned his radio down to a moderate volume, and waited to hear her rant. Surprisingly, she didn't say a word and began moving closer to the drivers seat. Javar figured he was going to get a kiss on the cheek until her head took a different direction. This was her way of apologizing, and he didn't stop her from leaning over to better position herself over his groin area. Neither of them said a word and went through her hard sucking and slobbing in silence, as he drove to their favorite spot, Ristorante Italiano.

Spreading his legs and relaxing in his seat gave Tasha more room to better craft her skill. Knowing She was excited, Javar lightly thrust his hips upward and added a slight circular motion. His palms began to sweat as he gripped the steering wheel tighter, running a stop sign in the process. She wanted him to give it to her, and Javar could no longer contain himself as her head bobbed faster, and her lips grew tighter around his erection. Swiftly sliding one hand up and down his mocha shaft, while gently massaging his balls, Tasha wished to share their contents.

"Fill my mouth up. I need an appetizer."

Thinking that She was the only one who could ever take all he had to offer, Javar released what Tasha wanted. As long as She was the one on his mind, the one that fulfilled his needs, he'd always do as She pleased.

Swallowing Tasha said, " Thank you. Baby, I'm sorry. I'll back off. I promise."

Many times when she spoke it was only for her to hear her voice. Javar ignored her apology for now, opting to think about how She would make it all better later.

After their lunch and dropping Tasha back at her office, Javar rode around thinking about the events in his life. He had some major decisions to make soon. Afterwards, peace would return.

Desperately needing to end things with Tasha had been on his mind for weeks. She had been so patient, loving, and understanding, but it was time to take his life to another level. There were so many avenues in the world for him to explore. She made him see that by opening his shut-eyes to his surroundings. She made it possible for him to be a voyeur, or participate if he so desired. Tasha was a wonderful girl, but there were no more buts. Tonight would be Javar's night - She had it already planned.

Arriving home a little earlier than usual, Javar was surprised to hear Tasha in their bedroom. Normally, he was always the first one to leave in the mornings, and the same followed suit in the evenings. Not wanting to do more talking than he had to, he began removing his clothing at the door, and was naked by the time he reached the bathroom.

"Javar, baby. Come here for a minute. I want to show you something."

Rolling his eyes and sighing, he walked his Adonis type nude body in her direction, stopping at the doorframe. The room was dimly lit with passion violet candles, and sexually scented with jasmine incense. Seeing Tasha on all fours with her ass in the air aroused him. She would be extra special tonight.

"What, Tasha? What do you want?"

"Now, baby. Need you ask? I want to feel you inside of me. You can take a shower afterward. Come' on...you know how I like it."

"I need to wash. I've had dried cum on me all day. I'll be back."

"Wash later. You're only going to get more on you. Be a good boy and get over here."

Growing tired of her cat like drone, he turned and walked back into the bathroom.

"Damn, that woman is sexy. I almost hate to do this to her but She leaves me no choice. After all that She's shown me, I have to move on."

Hearing the water flow from the shower was Tasha's indication to turn over on her back, and stretch her long legs upward to the ceiling as far as they could go. Pointing her toes aided in the effort of arching her back, while omitting sensuous sounds, and meowing like a kitten. Javar had been ignoring her in their bedroom repeatedly for the last few months, and Tasha wouldn't take it anymore. Tonight her lover would return.

Spreading her legs wide while running her hands over her smooth naked body would tantalize him. Not wanting to wait any longer, her desires called him.

"Javar, baby. How much longer are you going to be in the shower? I have a special gift for you."

Stepping out of the shower to hear her question he replied, "You know I have work to do. I don't have time for you tonight."

Sitting up while fondling her nipples Tasha concluded that Javar would not leave her alone again. "Work? Is that how you classify what you do? So it's work now?"

"Tasha, please. Not tonight. I'll be in the den if you need me."

The mood was broken for the moment but it would soon return. Knowing Javar would be hurt by her actions, Tasha pulled her legs in close, and wrapped her arms around her now fetal positioned body. Every since She came into their lives, their relationship had been on a decline. In order to get it back, She had to be taken care of.

"There is nothing that I won't do to show Javar it is I he needs, and nothing else. After tonight, She will no longer exist."

Screams of agony brought a seductive sneer to Tasha's face.

"Tasha! What have you done? Oh, no!"

Javar's anguished cries signaled Tasha to return to her position on all fours. He'd seen the busted screen on the computer monitor, the wires and the disk drives strewn about the room, and the keyboard ripped apart with some of the letters spelled out to read goodbye bitch. He would ask questions that he knew the answers to, and while Tasha answered them, Javar would be all hers.

While waiting on Javar to give her what She had been receiving, sweet, hot juices oozed from her. Finally, their lives were back to normal. She wouldn't be a problem any more.

C-Wrap

As she stepped from her car, Marisol thought about what she would say to Eva. After the T-Xtasy, things hadn't been the same between them. Marisol released her feelings through action and they were actually getting along, which was a slight shock to her. Sheila told her that she had let her attraction to Eva slip out, and Marisol thought that would make Eva's dislike of her progress further. Eva showed another side of herself by accepting Marisol's dinner invitations a few times, and hanging out with her every weekend after the T-Xtasy.

The T-Xtasy was a "party" like none of the three cohorts had attended before. The people that put on the H-Ball also planned the T-Xtasy, and their imaginations went beyond the realm of normalcy. The party was held in a warehouse that looked like a turkey pen. The rules were that you had to wear a costume made of feathers. The room was tight, and if you didn't want to get plucked, you simply should not have been there. The floor was covered with a large sponge-like material, so whenever the feeling hit, all the guests had to do was to assume a position.

As Eva was getting a few of her feathers removed by another guest, Marisol made her move. She walked up behind Eva and started pressing her body up against her back. Eva's partner continued arousing her from the front, and Marisol worked her sensuously from the back. She had decided that she would be the only one to stuff Eva that night. When the male figured out that his competition desired Eva more than he did, he backed off. The rest of the night Eva and Marisol teased and toyed with each other. The next day, a new friendship began to blossom.

It was one week before Christmas and the three of them made plans to wrap gifts over Eva's house. Marisol sashayed to the door holding her gift for Eva, which was wrapped in specially designed paper. She ordered it from an erotic gift supplier and arrived early so she could give her the gift in private. She pressed the bell seductively, and waited for her wish to come true.

"Hey, Marisol. Come on in. Is Sheila parking the car?"

Stepping across the threshold that she wanted to share she said, "No, we drove separately. I came early because I wanted to give you this."

After Eva opened the door she began walking in the direction of her den. Marisol's words and the sound of the lock clicking came out at the same time. She turned to face her.

"I hope you like it."

Marisol held a medium sized box. She extended her hands to Eva and smiled.

"I'm sure I will."

Eva pulled in a breath filled with mystery as she took the box. She noticed that the paper was a sexy design of Marisol in the nude.

"Marisol, uh, this paper is, uh…"

"Eva, I want you to be with me. Open the box."

Eva began biting her lip and light perspiration covered her neck. Her hands trembled slightly. She stared at Marisol intently and felt her throat beginning to burn.

"Eva, please…open the box."

Marisol's request was a soft sexy plea that Eva couldn't deny. Delicately she unwrapped the box. She couldn't help but stare at the nude pictures of Marisol on the paper. Her body was exquisite, but she said nothing. Once she had the wrapping off, she slowly opened the box.

"Oh, my...Marisol, I...I don't know what to say."

"Say nothing. Just let me do for you and you enjoy it."

The contents of the box were two tickets to Aruba, a set of keys to a condominium that Eva had spoken about, a cashier's check for ten thousand dollars, and a black lace see-through teddy.

Eva rolled her fingers around the teddy. She raised her head and took a few steps towards Marisol. As they began to lean into each other to kiss, the doorbell rang. Acting as if she were pulled to safety, she ran past Marisol to answer the door. Marisol dropped her head in defeat, and quickly began to gather the gift that Eva let fall to the floor. She had decided long ago that interruptions were only signs of what a promising future held. Her future promised her that she would hold Eva in her arms.

Soul Reverie

Uhm...Kelvin smells delicious. His commanding scent of summer ecstasy is exhilarating, intoxicating even. It's of no use for me to fight it. The euphoric aroma has ravaged my composure. I want him now.

I flung the water blue silk sheet from my body and began walking to the bathroom. The door was closed but with one simple push I'd conquer the man of my dreams. The cat and mouse games he plays with my emotions will be over soon. He is the one delicate delectable treat that always eludes me. He is the content of my sexual buffet that is always empty.

As my outstretched hand neared the door, it happened once again. The explosion I held for him came too soon. The hot, sticky feeling between my thighs beckoned me to awaken.

"Ahh...Just another wet dream. A dream that I'm sure would have quenched Kelvin's thirst."

For the last year, I, Connie Abrams, have secretly swooned over Kelvin Ridgeway. I work as a prosecuting trial lawyer and Kelvin joined the firm of Slauson and Thompkins as the receptionist. From the moment I saw him I fell in love. He stands a sleek model height of six-feet-two-inches, and has a body that summons my emotions to climax every time he walks past. His juicy lips drip nectar that has to be sweeter than any ever tasted from nature.

When I walk into the office there he is, sitting at the front desk looking sexier than the day before. I imagine my hands roaming through his wavy brown hair, and his doing the same to mine, while continuing to voyage down my body and lay comfortably in the small of my back. My body wants to hop over his desk and take control, taking him into my arms and releasing all of the sexual feelings I have pent up for him. Knowing he'll deny my advances I never make a move, and instead, greet him in the professional manner that he is accustomed to.

"Good morning, Mr. Ridgeway. Are you ready for a productive day?"

"Good morning, Miss Abrams. Of course I am. I always aim to please."

Then often times I stand like a mannequin reeling in his sensuality. Each day his cologne is different and my mind whimsically runs amuck trying to inhale him into my veins.

"Miss Abrams, are you alright?"

Sweat always soaks my collar and rolls down my back at the husky sound of his voice.

"Yeah...sorry. I was thinking about one of our clients. I'll talk to you later."

As I skirt away I usually see Kelvin staring at me with a confused, but always deliciously penetrating look on his face. I have to talk to myself to calm my obsession. Once I am safe and alone in my office, I drop my briefcase and run into my personal bathroom.

"Connie, girl, come' on. He's going to think you're an idiot. Just ask him out. What are you afraid of? It's a new era, a new millennium. Women are in control more than ever now."

As I watch my reflection in the mirror a slow prowling cheetah like shadow came up behind me. Kelvin wrapped his arms around my waist and I let out a low wanting gasp. He laid his head on my shoulders and then kissed me on my back, which electrified me through my blouse.

"Don't be so bashful, Connie. I know what you want and how to give it to you. I locked your door so we won't be interrupted. Shall I undress you?"

Unrestricted I answer, "Yes. You know exactly how I like it."

Kelvin spun me around to face him. He looked directly into my eyes before leaning in and circling his tongue around my mouth. He then eased his tongue in between my lips and kissed me with a fever that has no cure. I pulled him in close, pressing his chest into my breasts. My hands slid up and down his perfect silhouette, squeezing every inch of his flesh along the way. I felt a meteoric lift that I couldn't control and began to bend and lay him on the Persian carpeted floor.

Kelvin moaned, "Yes, yes. Don't be afraid."

As I kneeled to rest him on the floor I bumped my head on the counter top. Doing so returned me to the real world.

"What's happening to me? I can't handle a man like that."

If only for a few minutes I managed to shake off my feelings for Kelvin. Frantically, I tried to remain focused for the morning staff meeting. I did okay until my delightful dream buzzed my intercom.

"Yes, Mr. Ridgeway?"

His voice took hold of me and controlled me the same as an over-charged remote controlled car.

"Miss Abrams, Mr. John is in the conference room. He told me to let everyone know that he is ready to start the meeting."

I moved my hand down between my legs and gave the jumping participants a quick, but slow rub.

"Thanks, Mr. Ridgeway. I'll be right there."

As I stood to exit my office my hard nipples bumped a file that was hanging slightly off of the desk. I spoke to my tasty appetizers as I hurried into the meeting.

"Girls, you're going to have to relax. This isn't the time or place to show Kelvin how much I care for him."

They continued to throw a semi-tantrum but retreated in anticipation of an encounter with the man of my dreams.

I took the route to the room that didn't lead past Kelvin's desk. Looking at him and being unable to touch him is deafening to my heart. The very sight of Kelvin is long savoring. The taste of him is always in my buds, but the act of consuming his lusciousness evades me.

While sitting in a meeting devoid of any interest to me, I romanticized once again about Kelvin. In my imagined adoration I sat in a lounge chair at an island resort. A sweet breeze blew, which sent a light mist of my lover's fragrance and alerted me to a coming tryst. I sat up and saw him approaching holding a small platter of stimulating foods, and a bottle of champagne, with two flutes in his hands. Smiling, I lay back and waited the present of his body to me.

"That's it my love...just sit back. Let me take care of you."

I did as instructed and panted heavily as he straddled my pulsing moist body. He sat the bottle and flutes down at my side, and took an item from the tray for my pleasure.

"Open wide lover..."

With my eyes fixated on his face I opened my mouth to receive the first of many treats. A plump strawberry dripping with passion syrup made its way to my mouth. As it entered I sighed and bit down leisurely, allowing its juice to slide down my chin to my neck. Kelvin gladly obliged cleaning me up and began gliding his tongue over my blazing skin. Satisfied with the washing he took another appetizing menu item from the tray and fed me that as well. This time I received a slice of kiwi fruit that he quickly dipped in fluffed hazel cream. As the tempting treat exploded with flavor in my mouth, Kelvin licked the cream that landed on my lips off, and then pushed his tongue into my mouth to enjoy the essence.

"Oh baby…YES!" I moved my waist around in the leather office chair and professed my feelings for my fellow partners to hear. Most of them were prim straight-laced butt kissers and were startled by my sudden outburst.

Clearing his voice first my boss addressed me.

"Uhem…excuse me, Abrams. Would you like to include the rest of us in your meeting or would you like to join ours?"

Since I wasn't able to disappear in my embarrassment I blushed, which could easily be seen on my yellow plantain banana complexion. The legal pad in front of me that I hadn't written notes on was used as a fan that my hand spun on high.

"I'm sorry for the disruption, Mr. John. It won't happen again."

Clearly annoyed for losing his train of thought, he said, "See that it doesn't. Now where was I?"

His secretary cut a nasty look at me and then showed her mentor where he left off in his notes. Throughout the rest of the meeting I stole glances around the room and was happy that no one was looking at me. I tried hard to put all of my attention on Mr. John and the words he spoke. Silly smiles escaped me when Kelvin's face covered the face of the head senior partners'. There were no more disturbances, but at the end of the meeting Mr. John approached me.

"Abrams, follow me to my office, please."

The only time he had private meetings with his lawyers was if disciplinary action was to be taken or if you were terminated. I didn't think my interruption warranted either of those actions, but I was still nervous.

Mr. John walked around to his Lazy Boy style office chair and motioned for me to stand in front of his desk. He folded his arms across his chest while I took a soldiers stance and stood at attention.

"Abrams, I don't want to embarrass you by what I am about to say. Lately I've noticed that your mind and your eyes are wandering.

I stood stoic but was on the verge of panicking while my superior continued. "I don't condone fraternization among coworkers. It's not good for moral. People seem to forget why they're at work in the first place, but I like you Abrams. You're smart and you stay on top of your game."

My face lit up thinking I was about to receive a promotion. Instead, I received something much more endearing to my heart.

"I don't have a problem with women being the aggressor these days in relationships."

Beady eyes trailed my body from my head to waist. For the first time Mr. John saw me as a person with feelings and had to reorganize his thoughts before continuing.

"You have my permission to approach the man who is causing you to behave like a teenager in love. I know it's Mr. Ridgeway, and if he turns you down, I don't want to hear a word about it. Understand?"

It was a well-known hush-hush fact that Mr. John had affairs with every one of his personal secretaries. I wanted to tell him that Kelvin wouldn't be a plaything, but one day my husband.

"Thank you, Mr. John."

A nod was all I received before I turned and left his office. This time I didn't take the long route. I needed to see Kelvin in all of his workday grandeur. I walked up to his desk in reverse motion, replaying his sensuality over and over in my mind. When I stood two inches away from him he spun his chair around and telepathically pulled me into his waiting arms. We kissed fervently, with him sucking me deeper into his sensuous atmosphere. I held him tight, pressing my hands further and further into him, and giving firm squeezes that sent shock waves through my body.

He pulled his lips away for a moment.

"I love you, Connie."

Suddenly with acrobatic skill he swung my long legs around his muscular frame and I held on for the ride of my life. Kelvin lifted me up above his rigid area, opting to give it to me at the appropriate place.

"Miss Abrams are you okay? You look kind of faint. Can I get you anything?"

Once again my mind overpowered reality. I felt like an idiot and ran back to my office with profuse sweat dripping down my back. Once I was inside I slammed the door and dove to the floor, laying flat on my back for comfort.

"I have to control myself."

Looking down my horizontal body I saw my nipples rising again and I couldn't control my squirming legs.

"I can't, though. I'm going to ask him out before I go home. At least I'll know if he's interested."

The rest of my day was productive and upbeat. I conducted all of my business from my office and even ordered in lunch. The idea of stepping to Kelvin like a gentleman would a lady stayed in my mind, but instead of taking me on a sexual roller coaster, it pushed me to finish tasks on time.

As I tidied up my desk my private line rang. I assumed it was one of my girlfriends calling about the weekend tennis match and answered in my street voice.

"Yeah, holla at cha girl!"

"Excuse me?"

The papers I held went soaring across the desk. My heart ran down to my stomach and then criss-crossed behind me to return to my front. I fell into my chair and it rolled backwards a few inches, which caused the receiver to fall from my hands. I could hear the voice of a man calling me as it clunked on top of the desk, and then unraveled the cord as it dangled down the side of it. Trying to regroup quickly made me fall from the chair and slide face first under the desk. As I lay on the floor I grabbed the phone.

Almost screaming I said, "Hello! Hello! I'm here!"

The sound of his breaths drew me in.

Desperate and panting I asked, "Who is this?"

A brief pause of desire and then he spoke. "I'm the man of your dreams. Do you want me?"

In a whisper only enamored people could understand I responded.

"Kelvin? Is this you?"

"Yes, Connie. I know why you have been acting strange lately. I have been thinking of you, too."

Gradually I lifted myself off of the floor. My blouse had come out of my skirt and my necklace had come off and was halfway under the desk. I didn't care. He had received my internal messages of love and was attracted to me.

Lovingly I asked, "Where are you?"

"I'm at my desk. Every one has left except you. I couldn't take another day of not knowing how you felt about me."

"I'll be right out."

Stumbling a bit in my rushed movements I put myself back together and ran into the bathroom. I checked to make sure my clothing was in order and refreshed my breath with the secret stash of mouthwash I kept for this occasion. I took a few extra seconds to stop my trembling hands and then bound out of the office to finally connect with my sleep keeper.

I rounded the corner to Kelvin's desk and he stood to greet me. Biting down on the inside of my cheek helped me make sure that I wasn't imagining him. Wincing slightly from the pain I accepted that this encounter with him was real.

We extended our arms outward to give each other an inviting embrace. My eyes followed Kelvin's body from head to toe, paying special attention to the certain muscles he allowed me to see. We didn't speak any words as I reached him and pulled each other in close. My arms went up and around his neck and shoulders, and his went to my back and waist. I couldn't control myself any longer. My arms circled about as I pressed my face into his neck, inhaling his breaths as he exhaled.

"Connie, I've waited for this moment for so long."

My spirit opened up at the sound of his voice.

Seduction spoke.

"I can't wait. I want to go into the conference room. Take me there."

No questions were asked because we didn't need any answers. He picked me up and carried me to our temporary residence. I had kicked off my pumps somewhere down the hallway as I began to lose control.

"Kelvin..."

"Don't speak. Let me do all the work."

My dream was coming true. Most of the times I had visions of him I was the leader and he obeyed. There was a sofa in the room and I thought he'd head in that direction, but he walked over to the table and gently spread me on it buffet style.

My body lay open to him on the same table where the meeting was held earlier. I could see Kelvin from the side and he had taken off his clothing. Next I felt all of him sliding up my legs. He rose up when we were face to face and I looked downward at his body. I saw all that I had only previously imagined.

His entire body was robust and masculine. I ran my fingers through the light hairs on his chest as he moved in a light-titillating manner. Exhaling heavily relaxed me. He began unbuttoning my top and with each button, he kissed me. I lay in bewilderment. He reached the last button and splayed my blouse open to admire my succulent skin. Kelvin used his mouth to free my breasts and I began to blow short breaths out. He slid my skirt and stockings down, removed them, and never once lifted his hands from my body.

We were both totally nude in the workplace. Neither one of us cared. Kelvin climbed back on top of the table and slid his body up mine. I felt vibrations that rumbled from my nerves. My body tingled and thumped with each graze of his skin. Untouched sensors on my legs lifted to feel the marvelous creature that had entered our domain. Our bodies wanted to become one. Arms intertwined, legs wrapped tightly, chests meshed together to share worship that we had denied each other. Eyes locked into each other told the story of a love that was patterned by perfection. Each dream had orchestrated it.

I wanted this man. A Love Jones isn't real is what my friends said. They had never seen him because if they had, they would have categorized him as the one I'd been waiting for.

Between kisses I asked, "How did you know?"

Between kisses he replied, "A mutual love can never be hidden. I knew."

Then we spoke no more. I rode the dream wave to my truth. My truth of pleasing him and never letting him go. We pushed our bodies together gently at first and with each revelation of our hearts we went deeper. Kelvin held my body to brace us for the rush he let overwhelm him. His sweat dripped down on me. I licked its sweetness in and felt him in my psyche. We had joined without words. We used actions to celebrate.

Placing my hands on his waist I held him still. Our breaths halted as we took our relationship to another level. I knew he loved me. I released him to allow me into his world. Dreams ending with me alone didn't exist there. Kelvin took pleasure in showing me that he would be my live dream everyday.

"Kelvin, oh, Kelvin, yes...just like that."

He gave me what I requested.

My feelings left my body in euphoria. I had received the exhilaration that was missing from my daily naps. The delight that came from him was unexplainable. My language was incoherent but he understood.

The ride Kelvin took me on was smooth. If I went too high he took me back down to extend my pleasure. My toes curled and my lips twitched. My hands toured his body like a woman amazed.

The consummation was almost complete. Kelvin worked my body in such a way that I thought I couldn't take. After we'd finish making love in my dreams I'd sleep so soundly that sometimes I didn't hear the alarm clock. Kelvin made me want to sleep just to wake up to him again.

He requested, "Give me what you want me to have, baby."

I shared a year of unrequited desires. We held each other close, as not to waste what we desperately needed, and kissed tenderly as the elevated moment slowly dropped to ground level.

He laid his head on my chest and left kisses as our mood instructed. I closed and opened my eyes while taking deep reaffirming breaths. This moment had been the inspiration of my dreams. With my lips and tongue I traced Kelvin's face and pulled small sections of it in slowly, as not to remove it from his beautiful frame, into my mouth. I sucked it the same as an iced treat designed especially for me before I freed it.

"I can't believe I have you now."

My blockbuster dream responded. "Believe it. You shall have me for the rest of your life."

We carefully moved our bodies so we lay on our sides facing each other. The table was wide and held us both comfortably. For a few hours we held hands and talked excitedly about what the future held for us. We made more of my dreams come true before we heard the cleaning person jingling the keys trying to unlock a door that was barred with our hearts.

Some people may say that we submitted to each other too soon. Our respect for each other comes from deep within. We have been the source of one another's breaths throughout many nights. It doesn't matter to me if you call them dreams, trances, or imagined ideas. Kelvin was sent to me through my soul–for me, that makes our union a reverie that is real.

So Succulent

The day Mona mentioned bringing another woman into our bedroom was our third anniversary. We were in a passionate embrace, with her speaking softly in my ear all the things she wanted from me. As she whispered her desires, I circled my tongue on her neck. That was one of her spots and she'd moan that I was driving her insane.

"Stacy … Stacy, baby, let's have a threesome."

Hearing her say she fantasized about someone other than me came as a shock, and upset my mood. When I heard her words, I thought she was delirious. My tongue movement ceased as I slowly pulled away. Panting I asked, "What? What did you say?"

She stepped away from me and looked me square in my eyes. "I said, let's have a threesome. You wanna do it?"

Trying to contain my mild bewilderment I continued, "A threesome? A man? You want a man to have sex with you?"

The thought of bringing a man into our bedroom terrified me. If Mona had a tang of something so foreign and enjoyed it, she might up and leave me altogether. Not wanting to show my fear and insecurity I stood haphazardly poised, but cautious, while awaiting Mona's answer.

"No, Stacy. Hell no. What the fuck are we going to do with a man? I want a threesome with a woman."

Mona's eyes beamed as she talked about the member that would complete our triangle.

"This woman comes into the gallery every week and I think she'll do it. Every time I see her I picture her laying spread eagle on our bed with me on her face, and you lying on top of her tasting me."

As Mona finished her sentence, I heard something so sexy, so succulent, and so wet. It was she. The thought of the three of us together made her cum.

I was nervous, but didn't want to deny her wishes. "What's her name?"

"Succulent. Succulent Adams."

"Succulent Adams?"

"Well, every time she signs her credit receipt that's the name she writes. Succulent always physically touches me in some kind of way when I'm ringing up her items. I'm telling you, Stacy, that lady wants me."

"I don't doubt that she does, but what about me? Does she know you have someone in your life?"

"I'm sure she's seen my ring."

"A ring means nothing these days," was my nonchalant response.

Aggressively Mona continued, "Oh, Stacy. Lighten up. We don't have to do this if you don't want to. If she doesn't want the both of us then I'll drop it. Don't worry, baby, you're the only one for me."

The one thing that drew me to Mona was the fact that she never lied. There was no reason for her to start now, and no reason for me not to trust her. Feeling I needed her more now than ever, I moved closer to her and dove my tongue into her mouth. Mona wrapped her arms around my neck, jumped up and wrapped her legs around my torso. We pulsated our bodies against one another until our fervor could no longer contain itself.

"Stacy, baby. Give it to me now. Give me all you have to offer."

I lay down on our futon and descended Mona's seductively. Her breathing quickened in anticipation of what I'd do next. Her nipples were fat, erect, chocolate morsels. I devoured them as if I were the cookie that they belonged to.

"Ahhh, yes … oh, Stacy, yes, just like that, yes."

Mona's body emitted a sensuous heat that churned my obsession for her. I continued down her flaming body, sliding four of my fingers into her. The thought of another woman sharing our bed stayed in my mind. I felt I had to do whatever it took to keep Mona as my lady.

"Baby, do you want my tongue now?"

"You know I do. Please suck me … please."

Wanting Mona to crave only me, I abruptly stopped and said, "No. You've been a bad girl. Now get up and go to bed. This is your punishment."

Refusing sex is a game we often played with one another. Mona said no more and did as I commanded. She knew what was in store for her the next time and would do everything to make it worth the wait.

The next morning, Mona awoke before I did. I was a little worried my rejection in giving her what she wanted would backfire, seeing she'd been eyeing another woman, but I was incorrect.

"Stacy, you know you were wrong for cutting me off last night. Tonight, I'm going to make you pay."

A devious smile streaked across her face momentarily before she licked her lips and walked to the bathroom. I half wanted to join her, but decided to wait until that evening to see what she had planned.

While I was at work all I did was think about Mona and her interaction with Succulent. I couldn't control the jealousy that surrounded me either. The thought of the two of them talking, touching, and eyeing each other as if they were lovers bothered me. My thoughts got the best of me and as I reached for the phone to call Mona, it rang, which instantly pimpled my skin.

"Hello, Lingerie Lane–take a stroll with us and make all of your sexual fantasies come true. Stacy Roll speaking, how may I help you?"

"Hey, Stacy baby. Look, everything is all set. Meet me at Don Jens after work for drinks. Afterwards, we'll get a room or go home, okay?"

My skin's reaction was to break out in hives. I felt weak from the frantic stabs in my heart. I wasn't ready and let Mona know.

"After work today? Already? Damn, Mona. Can't we at least talk about this?"

"What's there to talk about? What's wrong? I thought you wanted to do this?"

"Well, yeah, but, ahhhh, um, I didn't think it would be tonight. What's your rush?"

Lustfully Mona said, "This is my revenge for last night. You owe me some good loving, and this is how I want it."

Mona knew I'd always give her what she wanted. I felt uneasy, but I agreed to her wishes.

"Alright, alright. I've just never done anything like this before. I'm a little anxious."

Soothing my nerves Mona added, "I love you, Stacy. Just wait and see. This is going to be wonderful."

"So ... Succulent knows about us? You told her you have a partner? How did she react? What did she say?" I fretfully asked.

"Calm down. She said she'd meet us after work. Don't worry, baby. Just relax and enjoy. A customer is coming in. I'll see you later. I love you."

Mona hung up before I could voice any more doubts. I didn't want to come across as old fashioned, but another person in the bedroom could be trouble. Should I change my mind and back out? Mona and I love each other. This wouldn't break us up, would it? Damn, I've already agreed to it. Mona would be hurt and think I didn't trust her if I back down now. Shit, let the games begin.

The door chime rang as soon as I hung up the phone. I looked up with a plan to put a smile on my face through my light sickness. Suddenly the room fell into a freaky haze and everything moved in slow motion. A being so damn fine walked towards me. My breath halted as my eyes froze on her. My body hadn't reacted this way to another woman since Mona. Was this considered cheating, looking or lusting? For me, it was all of the above. I'd fuck her real hard right now if she didn't tell.

Her stride was long and tempting. This woman had to stand at least six feet tall bare foot. Her six-inch heels made me want to climb to the mountaintop at that very moment and scream something more than the mere words my mind had consumed.

Words tripped over my tongue and my saliva trying to talk to her. "Hi ... hello ... ummm, welcome to Lingerie Lane. How can I fuck you?"

She smiled slow and said nothing. She was a team player. To me it didn't matter if her coach was a man or a woman; I just knew that she would hang in a scrimmage with me.

"I'm sorry, uhhh, that wasn't very professional of me. How can I help you?"

Her cleavage moved up and down. She had strategically placed a diamond pendant in the middle, which glistened the same as her abundant breasts. Mona has beautiful breasts, too. The two of them made me go wild ... what would four do?

She reached the counter and lay her bag down. A ring bursting with diamonds owned her middle finger on her right hand. I loved to see a woman with manicured hands and jewelry. This woman looked eloquent, not gaudy, and for some reason my hormones continued to rage.

"Yes, beautiful, you can fuck me anytime you want. Right now though, I would like for you to help me purchase a hot pink thong with matching nipple covers. I have a sexy date coming up, and I want my opponent to handle me with ease.

A team player that may be interested in a trade ... hmmm, if only for a season. Mona appeared and the thought of smacking this woman's ass, which I could see in the store mirrors, disappeared.

"We have what you're looking for right over here. Follow me."

I stepped from behind the counter and watched this fine ass Amazon follow me. Her legs were so long that I imagined myself holding on to one as I scaled to the top of it to reach my reward.

I stopped in front of the Sinfully Sexy display case. She stopped directly behind me and allowed her breasts to touch my back. She moaned aloud and I almost fainted. I hadn't thought of or touched another woman since Mona and I have been together. Lust is a bitch.

"Don't worry, beautiful. I didn't come here to cause any problems. I'll just take the pink set–size five, and be gone."

As I bent forward to remove the set from the case, she leaned into me. Her hotness penetrated through my clothes. I wanted to turn around and dive into ecstasy. My breathing grew slower and deeper, as if I were swallowing her through my nostrils. She did nothing to help my confused state of mind. She didn't move until I turned and handed her the too small covering for her stacked body.

"Thank you," was what she said as she took her purchase and walked back toward the counter. I felt an insatiable lust begin to slide down my leg. This was always done for Mona. Who was this woman?

"Uh, Miss, you are the recipient of today's special. All pink sets are free. Here's a bag for your lingerie. Please come back and tell all of your friends."

My attempt to regroup and sound professional was idiotic at best. She stopped, took the bag from me, and then slid her tongue into my mouth. Her intrusion turned into a long, slow kiss. I reached up and caressed her breasts. She stepped in closer and I placed my naughty hands around her ass. It was so soft–I wanted to palm it, then smack it, and watch it shake.

Miss Amazon pulled away from me. "I'll see you next week, beautiful."

I stood in the middle of my boutique and watched my fantasy walk away. The way that I felt didn't make any sense to me. Easily I would have gotten naked for that woman. My mind thought of Mona. Did I behave that way because I now knew she had been looking at another woman or was I simply an ass?

The remainder of the day was hectic. I thought of Mona and the night she had planned, and tried not to think of the woman who made me not think of Mona. My senses ran crazy. Hennessy VSOP was the only thing that calmed me, so I closed up the shop forty-five minutes early and began my ride to Don Jens. Mona and I weren't supposed to meet there for another ten minutes, but I saw her car when I pulled into the lot. I wanted to ram into it for making me misbehave, but I parked in the space next to it instead. As I walked up to the entrance, I hesitated. After seeing Mona entwined in a deep conversation with the ravishing woman who came into the boutique I continued. She was gorgeous. I slowed down to see what I had missed earlier. Her silky straight black hair hung past her shoulders. Automatically, looked at her long neck and booming cleavage that I'd fondled. Her lips were pouty, and her eyes endearing and dark.

The hostess greeted me at the door with welcoming words that were not understandable in my nervous state. I rushed past her in the direction of their table, realizing that I had to try hard to not sound ruffled or worried when I spoke. Mona saved me from both.

"Ahh, here's my baby. Stacy, this is Succulent. I took the liberty of ordering Hennessey VSOP and the spinach dip appetizer."

Succulent slid over in the booth and patted the cushion next to her. Mona gave a nod, and I sat down. Succulent's aroma was a soft cherry mist that commanded my actions with each breath. She placed her long slender hand on my thigh, and   slowly, squeezed it before she spoke.

"So, you're Stacy. Mona's told me all about you. She really loves you and I can see why."

Succulent didn't let on that she and I had met. I didn't want to feel like I was hiding something from Mona, and began to tell of the afternoon tryst. Succulent sensed that I was about to blurt it out and placed her finger over my mouth. She slid it back and forth and then gently sucked it inside.

Mona began to rotate in her seat. I sat still, entranced that my baby was so excited by this. Succulent removed her finger from my mouth and placed it in hers.

"Mmmm, Mona, Stacy is delicious. Thank you for allowing me to share."

I glanced over at Mona and blew her a kiss. Suddenly, I realized that this evening was going to be good. Very, very, good.

The waitress returned with our drinks and appetizers. Succulent lifted my glass, let it touch my lips, and then set the glass on the table. Her lips instantly met mine. I hesitated, but relaxed when I felt Mona's foot sliding between my legs.

The fact that we were in a public place is what stopped us. We pulled back and enjoyed a dinner of vinaigrette tossed romaine salad, chicken fettuccine, stuffed mushrooms and mozzarella rolls. During our dinner conversation Succulent revealed a few tidbits of who she was, but kept me guessing on where she came from, and how in the hell she got to be so fine.

"Ladies, I'm an exotic dancer. The funny thing is, my birth name is Succulent Adams. I enjoy life, I enjoy people and I enjoy experiences. Besides that, there is nothing spectacular about me. Now that the formalities are out of the way, where shall we begin?" Succulent said this in a captivating tone, which put me more at ease.

"We can go to our place. It's not too far from here and you can spend the night afterwards if you like."

I couldn't believe I jumped in like that, but it brought a smile to Mona's face. Surprisingly, I was more ready than I thought.

Mona told Succulent to ride with me. She talked while feeling me up as I drove.

"Stacy, you have nothing to worry about. What happened this afternoon is cool. I'll never tell. Having an attraction in life is okay. I know you love Mona and I don't want to get with her past tonight unless it's the three of us. I do find her very attractive, but that's where my interest stops. The three of us doing this is all about sex for me. Just sexual pleasure, okay? Can you handle that?"

Confidently I said, "Okay. I can handle it. I love Mona and want our relationship to work. I don't know what got into me this afternoon, but I can never do anything like that again."

"This afternoon was a test for tonight. I heard Mona talking to you once on the phone when I was in the gallery. I knew she planned for us to meet tonight. You had to see if you could do this, that's all. That's why I placed myself in your court. You were just testing yourself … you don't want me."

I said no more. Hormones, lust, or a test. I couldn't think anymore. We were five minutes from home and at this point, it didn't matter.

Mona came home earlier and spruced up our place. All of the light bulbs had been changed to red or blue, potpourri sachets were hung in every room, and extra candles were placed in the bedroom. Soft music played as we entered our loft, which gave an erotic, radiant ambiance.

"Okay, ladies. There's no need for anymore talking. Let's disrobe here and go take a shower."

As Mona was speaking she was also taking off her clothes. Succulent and I joined in, and the three of us walked naked into the bathroom. I purposely walked last to get a good look at Succulent. Mona would never lose my love, but Succulent was stunning. Her breasts were perfectly plump, which made them sit up on their own, and her legs were track star toned, long and slender, with delicious looking feet carrying it all.

Mona turned on the shower and stepped in, standing in the middle. Succulent stepped in next and stood farthest from the showerhead, and then I got in. Mona turned towards me and we kissed like it was our first time, releasing our devotion in the hot steam as the water danced off our bodies in an ideal rhythm.

Succulent pulled her body up behind Mona, and reached her arms around to touch her and my breasts. In unison, we gyrated our bodies slowly, slithering up and down each other, using the water as a lubricant. Mona reached behind me to grab the body gel and squeezed it all over us. Still in unison, our hands roamed over each other's bodies in precise movements, becoming familiar with what we soon would share in depth.

Mona then placed me in the middle and turned me towards Succulent. Our voyage continued with Succulent nibbling my face and slipping her tongue into my mouth, which better acquainted the two of us.

"Ah, Mona. You didn't tell me Stacy was so sweet. Mmmm."

I lay my head back on Mona's shoulder as Succulent glided down my body and entered me with her tongue. As Succulent tasted me wholeheartedly, Mona caressed my breasts and kissed my neck. She whispered low, pleasing words in my ear, satisfying me the entire time.

"Do you like this Stacy? Does it feel good?"

"Uh-huh. Ah, yes. Uh-huh."

We continued our shower ritual for another fifteen to twenty minutes. Without breaking the mood, Mona turned off the water and moaned, "Let's grab towels and head to the bedroom."

Succulent and I obeyed like hungry pedigree dogs. In the bedroom, Mona instructed us on what to do next.

"Stacy, lay on your back and spread them wide so I can see everything. Succulent, enjoy my buffet and I'll take care of you."

We all lay on the floor in the positions Mona instructed, which ended up looking like a chocolate train.

Mona was definitely the ringleader and informed us when the ride was complete to get into the bed. This is what she had been waiting for. Succulent lay on her back and Mona sat on her face. I lay on top of Succulent and fingered her, while I savored Mona's sweet ass in the process.

"Oh yeah, Stacy … only you know what I like …"

After Mona's release we switched positions. She lay on the bed and Succulent eased her body on top of her with me sitting on Mona's face. Mona's tongue inside of me was more intense—if the moment had a comprehendible voice, it would say the sincerest thank you and more.

The highlight of the evening came when Mona asked to watch me and Succulent. Never denying Mona, I obliged. I began by sucking her lavish breasts, and everything in between them and her Brazilian waxed region. I rode her softly with my body and my fingers. She reciprocated, which made Mona scream with delight.

Although I was enjoying myself, I didn't want to watch Mona and Succulent make love. I wasn't ready for that. Succulent watched Mona and I, and once again, Succulent and I gave Mona a show. Mona must have sensed my apprehension and only touched Succulent if the three of us were involved.

Succulent left us satisfied at 2:30 a.m. She was ready for more action and decided to take a taxi to the club where she worked. We all kissed at the door; with Succulent saying whenever we needed a refresher she'd be ready. The evening was sinful and I do believe that I would be with Succulent again if Mona desired it. With that silent thought, I was glad that Mona didn't plan another date. I wanted her all to myself each and every time we made love.

Mona and I walked back to the bedroom hand in hand, and looked at our wet sheets, smiling at what we had just experienced.

"Stacy, thank you for allowing me to do this. It was wonderful."

"Yes it was. I had my doubts, but you relaxed me. I love you."

As Mona and I lay back in our bed she rolled over on top of me. I wanted Mona, and I began to show her she'd be mine forever. My imagination placed Succulent in our bed, and I wondered would I ever see her again.

One Night Stand...Or Two

Delvina Harris reluctantly planned to spend another Friday night alone. She dreaded staring at the television set, and eating junk food that had been scattered all around the house during the week. The local movie rental store was her best friend as she had just come in with the latest releases, but was in no hurry to watch them.

For most of her existence, Delvina had been on a serious mission to find someone to share her life with. She was a thirty-five year old plus-sized voluptuous woman who held her beauty well. All of her friends and family told her this, but she longed to hear more than just those menial compliments from one special man. Every man she went after always told her he was flattered and then added that she really wasn't his type. The last man she approached, Trent Mills, hurt her feelings the same polite way—whatever that is.

While the microwave popcorn jumped into a frenzy, Delvina grabbed an opened bag of stale cheese doodles off the kitchen counter. They'd been sitting there since Monday, and since she was taught not to waste food, she ate them anyway. She then went into her den and spread her movie choices for the night on the coffee table.

"Let's see, hmm, I think I'll start with this horror flick, then the comedy, and last but not least, the love story. Maybe it will have a good sex scene in it and I'll go to bed happy. Who says a big girl can't get any satisfaction?"

Sighing at the sound of her flesh as it plopped down on the dented sofa, she sat back and desperately wished she had someone to share her life with. Another evening alone was depressing. She knew her weight was a problem, but a man should love her for who she really was.

"I guess all that fairy tale stuff happens in the soaps and on one hour talk shows. Well, the hell with them. I'm a good woman and one day, I'll have a chance to give my love to the right man."

The microwave buzzer went off and Delvina walked listlessly into the kitchen. She inhaled the smell of burnt popcorn, grabbed the piping hot bag, a three-liter bottle of soda, and took the same listless steps back into her den.

"Here's to another fantastic night."

Her evening was toasted by turning up the bottle of soda and taking a large swig. She pressed play on the DVD remote and stuffed her mouth with the popcorn. Halfway through the movie she'd finished the bag, the soda, and the extra supply of goodies she had by her side, and wished she had something else to do.

Thinking back on her man activity made her shake her head in disgust. She stared at the TV and saw her last two male encounters fill up the screen.

One day she had the brilliant idea to join a health club in an attempt to meet men. Although she was pushing a size twenty-six, she never was attracted to big men. She wanted a nice, toned, handsome muscular man who could sweep her off her feet and make love to her like in romance novels. On her first day in the gym, before she even began a workout routine, she walked up to Trent and let him know exactly how she felt about him.

"Excuse me, sir. I came in here to work on my lotta body, but I can't begin without introducing myself to the most gorgeous man in here. My name is Delvina, and I'd like for us to become friends. Is that possible?"

Trent looked around the gym as if she were speaking to someone else, and continued with his exercise routine of walking on the treadmill. Delvina gave a little huff, tapped him on the shoulder, and rephrased her request.

"Sir, sir. I'm speaking to you. I can come back when you're finished, but I'd like to know your name. Is that possible?"

Trent slowed down his pace, looked around the room again, and gave her a crooked smile before speaking.

"I'm Trent Mills. But look, deviled eggs, or whatever your name is. I'm not here to get hit on by women. Your approaching me is very flattering but I think you need to go do what you came to do. Hit me back in a year or two; if your body matches your face, I'll think about it."

Instead of her making a comment in her favor she turned and walked out of the gym. Trent spoke very loud and the three people on treadmills next to him heard every word. They couldn't contain their snickers, and Delvina couldn't contain her embarrassment, or put on a fake front and exercise. The event with Trent happened two years ago and that was the last time she'd set foot in a gym.

When she was twenty-three, she went on a date with Mark Hughes, a man she worked with and was also three sizes larger than she. Delvina was a size twenty-two back then and was horny enough to do anything. She didn't bother to take the time to get to know Mark and instead, hopped into bed with him on their first date.

What a disaster that was. Mark failed to inform her that he liked to have sex while pretending to be a wild bear that was mauling his victim. Delvina continued with the intercourse because she actually liked the way he felt, but as soon as she reached an orgasm, she jumped out the bed, got dressed, and listened to Mark rant and rave about how he was hungry and she couldn't leave yet.

When she arrived home, Mark had filled her answering machine up with loud snorts, smacking noises, and pleas for her to come back and finish what they started. Needless to say, that was the last time she spoke to him, and the last time she'd had sex.

Her eyes returned to the horror movie, but her ringing telephone saved her from the weak screams of the latest victim.

"Thank, God. Maybe this is my knight in shining armor calling to apologize for leaving me alone all these years. Hello?"

"Dee, got a minute?"

"Oh, hey, Jerry. Yeah. What's up?"

Jerry was Delvina's first cousin. They'd been pushed together since birth and he was the one person she was close to. Jerry annoyed her at times because he always had a get rich quick scheme that he needed her money to invest in, or a woman that he wanted her to approach for him. None of that mattered this time, though. Jerry was a wonderful reprieve from her movie so she put it on pause, and listened eagerly to her saving grace.

"There's a party down at the Aces Lounge tonight and I need you to be my escort. Samantha Davis is going to be there and I need a little help in showing her I'm sincere. Are you game?"

"Umph. Samantha Davis, huh? Hasn't she turned you down numerous times before? Isn't she engaged?"

"As long as she ain't married I still have a chance. Tonight will be the perfect night for us to hook up. Her man is out of town on business and I know she's lonely. Come' on, get ready. I'll pick you up."

Looking at the ceiling she responded with, "Oh, Jerry. That girl isn't even thinking about you. And how do you know she'll be there anyway?"

"She told me. She likes me to chase her and I'm not tired of running yet. Samantha is fine. She's only engaged to that fool because he has money," was Jerry's flip attitude reply.

"Well, no woman wants a broke man."

"True, true. I'll have my fortune one day but until then, I just want her by my side. Now get ready. I'll be there in thirty minutes."

"Wait a minute. What am I supposed to do while you're wooing Samantha? You know I always end up sitting alone being bored. I don't feel like getting dissed tonight."

With as much love as he could muster over the phone Jerry boomed, "Delvina, you know I love you, but you need to get off your 'nobody loves me' soap box. What are you doing now? Watching movies and eating, right?"

After a five second teeth-suck, with a slouch she managed to say, "Yeah, right."

"How are you going to get a man if you don't start treating your body better? I'm not saying you can't get a man at your size, but at least make an effort to be more healthy. You expect the perfect man to fall in your lap when you aren't offering anything near the perfect woman. Now get ready; I'll be there soon."

"Alright. See ya soon."

"That's my girl. I love you. Bye."

Jerry hung up before she could respond. She held the receiver for a moment and smiled. Jerry was irritating at times, but at least he was always honest.

She stood up and looked at herself in the full-length mirror outside her bathroom door. She did look rather sloppy in linty black stretch pants and an oversized wrinkled shirt that had a few stains on it. She didn't bother to spray her wrapped hair this morning after she untied it and it was quite dry.

"Damn, girl. This is nowhere near the fly girl you are. Get a grip."

Delvina continued to stare at herself in the mirror while running her fingers through her hair. When she noticed a cheeto crumb stuck to her lip she shook her head and decided she'd get herself together starting now.

"I'm a beautiful woman; and tonight, I'll show someone just how good I can be."

After a long hot shower Delvina decide to wear a form fitting knee-high red dress with the back out. She'd purchased it three months ago but never got up enough nerve to wear it, seeing she hadn't lost any weight. Her skin rolls showed in the back, and for once, she didn't care. She did her best to put glitter lotion on her flabby areas and stepped out of her bedroom looking physically the same, but with a more positive attitude.

There was nothing that disgusted her after she gave herself a once over in the mirror. Her wrapped hair was back to its bouncy, shining, sleek look, her make-up was on and tight in all areas, and her dress fit better that she remembered. She strutted to the sofa with confidence and sat down like she'd just finished a Paris photo shoot. While waiting for Jerry, she ran her hands over her smooth legs, and put on her calf tie red sling backs. Just as she finished lacing up her right leg, Jerry lay on the doorbell and called her name like he had no manners.

"Delvina! Girl, get out here! I got a woman waiting on me! Let's go!"

She grabbed her purse and walked to the door with a sexy high strut. Once Jerry saw her she was sure he'd change his tone. She swung the door open with a smile on her face and said nothing more.

Jerry's eyes lit up and his mouth fell open. He smiled and responded with gibberish that was actually a compliment.

"Holy shit, Dee! Damn, whoa, oh, damn."

"Yeah, I thought you'd say that. Now keep it down and let's go. There's a man I need to meet."

"Now that's what I'm talking 'bout. That's the Delvina I know. Give me a kiss before I have to wait in line."

Delvina and Jerry laughed and gave each other a hug while he pecked her on the cheek.

"Girl, you smell good. What is that you're wearing?"

"It's called One Night Stand. Now quit yapping and start driving. I'm ready for tonight."

"Oh shit. Whatever you desire, my lady. Whatever you desire."

They high-fived each other before getting into Jerry's car and talked about who and what they would conquer tonight at the lounge. Jerry did most of the talking as Delvina saw herself being kissed and caressed by Mister Do-Right. She couldn't see his face clearly, but his body meshed with hers. She felt herself getting wet and mistakenly moaned out loud at the thought of a large sexy man entering her.

Jerry slowed down a little before looking at his cousin. He wasn't surprised because he knew she was ready to give herself to one man totally.

"Where yo' mind at? You horny or something?"

Slightly embarrassed, but glad it was Jerry who heard her, she said, "Oh, sorry. Hell yeah I'm horny. A big girl needs extra love and I'm way behind. I'm not leaving this club tonight without some hard sumthin' sumthin' by my side."

"Slow it down, cuz. You know how some brothas' can be. I mean, I think you're beautiful, but some men are only concerned with looks."

"Who said it had to be a brotha'?" She turned her lip up and sat back ready to ride.

"Damn. Are you about to cross over? I guess you really are horny."

"Look, a dick is a dick. I'm not in it for the color, just the size and hardness. If it happens to be attached to someone of a different race then...."

"Okay, I'll give you that. But you know what they say about the brothas'?"

"No what?"

"Girl, you know about the big feet and big hands? It equals size."

Jerry gave his I'm so sure look as if he was talking about himself. Delvina responded with a serious hand signal and a neck roll to match.

"The only thing a black man with big feet or hands has is big feet or hands. I haven't been around, but I've heard women talk. The black man's anatomy isn't all that. Sorry to crush you."

"I'm not even going to justify that shit. Besides, we're here, Miss One Night Stand."

Softening her tone would be her apology.

"You'd better get ready for, Samantha. Don't worry about the black man's anatomy either; I heard you had it going on."

His frown flipped quickly and his eyes lit up.

"Who told you about the J-man?"

Delvina laughed and patted Jerry on his thigh. She loved her cousin for always bringing a smile to her face.

"Let's go. Your anatomy can't do a thing for me. Besides, Mister Do-Right is waiting."

"Now, that's what I'm talking bout'. Samantha, here I come baby."

She laughed at his comment and then exited the car looking more confident and feeling surer of herself than when they left her home. She knew rejection would probably play a big part in her game tonight but she was adamant it wouldn't win.

Jerry took her hand as they entered the Ace's Lounge. Even though she looked more confident on the outside, he still felt he had to help her along on the inside. He loved his cousin and didn't want her to get hurt. He planned to cheer her on from the sidelines with whomever she chose for the night.

They found a cozy little table near the bar and as Delvina sat down and got comfortable, Jerry went and placed orders for their liquid pleasures.

As she sat silently she scoped out the medium sized bar for her prey. She was seated in a spot in which she could see the lounge from all angles, and scanned the room slowly as not to miss a thing. She didn't hear Jerry as he came to the table, placed her drink in front of her, and sat down. Delvina could only concentrate on the sound of bingo in her head, and the fine tall man that stood directly in her view.

"Hey, cuz. Come out of that trance. Here's your drink."

Delvina didn't reply to Jerry, but nodded slightly instead. She was afraid if she turned her head she'd miss her chance with Mister Do-Right.

As if it were he who hit pay dirt Jerry exclaimed, "Oh, shit! Do you have your eye on somebody already? Damn, girl. We just got here. Who is it?"

Cautiously she asked, "Who is that man over there by the DJ booth? Please tell me his name."

Jerry looked in the same direction as she and began to smirk. He knew exactly who she was looking at, and knew why she was attracted to him. All the women were attracted to him.

Alex B. Not his real name, but a name that drove many ladies wild with interest. Alex stood six-feet-two inches tall and had a sculptured body frame to go along with his height. He had a medium muscular build, and a very voracious sexual aurora about him. Every woman that looked into his dark piercing eyes always wanted more, and did everything in her power to get it.

Alex was part owner of the Aces Lounge and was at the bar every night. He always came alone, but never left without two or more women on his arms. There was no way Jerry would let Delvina be used by him.

"No can do, cuz. That's the biggest player in here. All he wants is pussy and nothing more. I thought you wanted a meaningful relationship with someone? Don't bother with him."

"Jerry, I told you tonight was all about me getting laid. With all this stuff I got, humph, he can play me all night long."

"Look, Dee. I know Alex isn't your type. He thinks he's the shit because he owns this bar. He's very superficial and only likes women that look like they come from nudie magazines. Don't waste your time."

Not listening to Jerry and debating her cause was the only thing on her mind.

"All I have is time. Making an introduction won't hurt will it? Maybe it's time for him to try something new. Maybe it's time for him to try me."

Jerry turned and faced Delvina. When he saw the sparkle in her eyes that he hadn't seen in years, he decided to say no more. He didn't want to see her hurt, and somehow felt he wouldn't.

"Well, I guess your mind is made up. You want me to introduce you to him?"

"No. I can handle this on my own. You go and find Samantha. Oh, and Jerry…if you don't see me at the end of the night, don't worry about it. I'll be fine."

Jerry picked up his drink, gave her a kiss on her cheek and went off to find his woman. He spotted Samantha a few feet in front of him and picked up his step to get closer to her. Delvina glanced around to see him looking like a pimp from the seventies going to meet his bitch.

"Oh, Jerry. What am I going to do with you," is all she could say as she giggled to herself. She quickly returned her eyes back to Alex. Damn he was sexy.

"I bet he's excellent in bed, too. I can't wait. I have to find out."

Delvina gulped her rather tall drink of a Long Island Iced Tea down and tried to look seductive as she wiped the spill-over off the sides of her mouth. She then stood up, smoothed her dress, and began taking slow long steps over to Alex. He was still standing by the DJ booth, viewing the room and giving it his approval. His body swayed seductively with the beat, so he didn't notice as she walked up and stood next to him. Only when she bumped his side with her elbow did he acknowledge her with a slight nod. He then returned to his sway, and did nothing more.

He's gorgeous up close. And uhm, uhm, uhm, the smell on him. Oh, yes, yes. Make him your lover tonight.

"Uh, excuse me, Alex, right? My name is, Delvina. I just had to introduce myself to the owner of this fine establishment. The Aces Lounge is very nice."

Flashing his million-dollar playa smile was his first move. Speaking in a low voice was the next.

"Delvina, that's an interesting name. I've never seen you in here before. Do you like the atmosphere?"

She felt herself tense up at the sound of his voice. He had to be a quiet storm midnight disc jockey. He voice would be wasted otherwise.

"Yes, your place is very nice. I'm sorry I didn't come here sooner."

"Not to worry. This club isn't going anywhere. You can come back as much as you like."

Damn he's turning me on. Do I make my move now? Will I look like a fool? Will I look desperate? It's still early. Maybe he won't want to leave. Maybe he'll tell me where to take my fat ass. Fuck it. It's now, not never.

"May I be honest with you?"

Alex continued looking straight ahead as he responded. "Yes."

"I came here on a mission. I came here looking for a man to bed tonight. I came here looking for you."

Alex didn't shift his glance to her after her comment. He continued to sway to the music and motioned for the waitress to come over for his drink order.

Beginning to feel stupid, Delvina wished she'd thought more about her plan of attack. Deciding to walk away instead of embarrassing herself any longer, she took a step in the direction of the ladies room as the waitress approached to take his order.

"Delvina, what would you like to drink?"

She stopped in her tracks and flashed a beaming smile at Alex.

"I'll have a Long Island Iced Tea. Thank you."

"Ahhh, a woman after my own heart. Make that two, Candy. And, Delvina, you're welcome."

Candy smiled at Delvina and walked away. She stepped back in her original position next to him and began to sway, also.

Facing Delvina, Alex looked her directly in her eyes.

"I noticed you were going to walk away. Were you going to leave me standing here all alone?"

Meekly she replied, "Uh, yeah. You didn't respond so I figured you weren't interested. Are you?"

"Well, I'll be honest with you. At first, no. I don't mean to be rude or shallow, but I've never been with a woman larger than a size eight. I like what I like and I'm sure you do as well."

"So why did you change your mind?"

"I don't know actually. You're beyond beautiful and your straight forwardness excites me. Many women approach me but none are as honest as you. I think we can talk."

Candy returned with their drink orders and stood next to Alex momentarily. Delvina got the gist that the two of them had a thing going on, but not tonight. Alex showed and inch of interest in her and Delvina would not stop until she had the whole nine yards and more.

Whatever Alex whispered to Candy made her frown her face up and walk off in a huff. He then turned his attentions to Delvina by asking many questions she had the answers to.

"So tell me? What do you want to do to me, and what do you want in return?"

Delvina took a sip of her drink, this time more relaxed and mysterious, and answered his questions with the confidence she had.

"I'll start by saying I know I'm a big girl. That just means you'll get big love. I can take your body everywhere at the same time and make you feel ooh, so good. I can take any amount of dick you have anywhere in my body and make you feel ooh, so good. I can rub your body down, make it come back up, and all the while make you feel ooh, so good. It's not about what I want; it's about what I want you to have. Now how about we go to my place and get started."

By that time Alex had his eyes locked in on her face. He watched her lip movements and every time she spoke he grew more erect. He held his drink at his mouth but never took a sip. It was as if he was mesmerized by her words, and would do anything she asked.

"Uh, I have to take care of a few things here, and then we can leave. Go wait by the door; I'll be there in five minutes," Alex said through a sexy smile.

He bent and kissed Delvina on her lips before he turned and walked away. By that time, they had an audience of women watching and they all went into a gossiping frenzy. She finished her drink, placed the empty glass on the table next to her, and walked to the door with high steps. She switched fiercer than she'd ever done before, and dared any woman to say something to her. She was ready for Alex. She deserved this. And she'd let any woman know this was her turn and her night.

Delvina reached the door and saw Jerry on the dance floor with Samantha. He looked in her direction and gave her thumbs up. Delvina responded with the, 'I'll call you signal', as Alex approached.

"A friend of yours?"

"My cousin, Jerry. I was letting him know that I was leaving. All set?"

"Yes. Follow me."

Alex placed Delvina's hand in his softly and led her to his black Navigator. He opened the passenger door and helped her step up and in. He then slid in a CD of jazz classics and gave her another kiss before he pulled off. They rode to her place with Delvina sitting close to him, and Alex offering a kiss at each stoplight.

Parking in the driveway made her ecstatic. She couldn't believe he was at her place and knew it was no talk show. He helped her out of the car and they strolled in through the front door and straight to her bedroom.

"Have a seat on the bed, Alex. I'll be right back." Gliding, she gathered some candles and bought in a bottle of wine and glasses. She lit the candles, turned on her radio to the quiet storm mix, and sat next to him.

Handing Alex the bottle she asked, "Would you do the honors?"

"Sure."

He opened the wine and poured a glass for the both of them. Before he made a toast he placed the bottle on the nightstand and thought about the wonderful night ahead.

"This is to new beginnings, experiences and friends."

"Hey now..."

They gently clinked their glasses and took a sip. After looking into each other's eyes they began to kiss.

"Wait, Alex. Let's make you comfortable." Delvina placed both glasses on the nightstand and began to undress him. She made sure all of her movements were slow and sexy, and kissed Alex with each button she undid. He wore a navy blue blazer with a matching shirt and when she reached the last button, she ran her fingers up and down his smooth hairy chest.

"I feel good already."

"I know, baby. Just relax."

She slid his jacket and shirt off his arms and dropped it to the floor. While undoing his belt and trouser zipper she kissed him again, and then placed her hand inside his pants, feeling his erection that was waiting to get inside of her. She stroked it gently, while listening to his delightful moans of pleasure.

"Alex, baby. Stand up a minute so I can see all you have to offer."

He obliged and she slid his pants and boxers down to the floor. He stepped out of them and embraced Delvina tightly. Their tongues teased one another while they learned the layout of each other's body with their hands.

"Sit down...I wanna show you something."

He sat back on the bed and watched her undress in front of him. The quiet storm helped her. Toni Braxton's Making Me High induced the room and Delvina began working for imaginary money. Alex swallowed and everything hardened on him as he watched. He sang the song low and she worked to keep his words coming. Her hips moved seductively and slow from side to side. Then she lifted one leg, placing it on the bed to the side of him, and undid one shoe. When she bent to slide it off her foot her breast touched his face. She said nothing as he kissed it and stood up to see him enthralled by her movements.

"Do you like what you see, baby? Am I turning you on?"

He said nothing and his eyes grew wide. For a moment, he looked like cocaine was his king. She continued wiggling and rotating her body on a pole that should have been there. Dropping to the floor her ass moved forward and back, and then sensuously swayed side to side as she eased back up. Alex stroked himself in a room that was a tidal wave of chocolate motion. He, the smooth, dark, sinfully delicious middle to Delvina's round, soft, delicate exterior, waiting to envelope him and become a sweet desert of indulgence.

"That's it, baby. Get him ready for me."

She raised her other foot up and removed it in the same manner as the first one. Her only customer watched in amazement. This time he kissed and sucked her breast. When she turned to watch him she replaced her breast with her lips. He kissed her passionately and grabbed her waist.

"Wait, baby. Let me give you a full view."

Delvina backed away from him and lifted her left leg while rotating her ass and hips. Clockwise she went, stopping all time as Alex and her became more intimately acquainted. Up and down her leg went—her hips rolled like a butter churner as she revolved around and around. An imaginary hula-hoop kept her pace. With her arms raised above her head she turned. Her head lay back as sensuous beads moved in her mind. Swish, swish, swish…slowly she swished. The voice in her head told her to work it and work it well.

The swishing halted momentarily when Delvina stopped with her back towards Alex. She bent down slowly, and pushed her ass out for him. From side to side she began to rock, and added a slight up and down angle bounce. She wanted him to think of her as an all you can eat hot cross bun. A mound of temptation – moist – sweet – dark – sticky...nothing that would harm him, but enough to make him hurt himself trying to take it all in.

Swish, swish, swish was all she heard when she stood and began to turn. When she was facing Alex again his posture was bent forward with his hands reaching out. He wanted her. She took a step back and grinded hard and slow as she slid her dress off. When her dress hit the floor, she reached back and undid her bra, unleashing her forty-four C's, and letting them fall above her waist. She then bent to take off her silk panties and stood in silence to let him see exactly what he had gotten himself in to.

"Am I too much for you?"

A few seconds passed before he could speak.

"Hell no. Damn you got some big pretty titties. Come here."

She straddled him and let her breasts fall in his face. Alex went wild with excitement, trying to kiss and suck the both of them at the same time. He ran his hands all around her body and never once removed his mouth from her breasts.

"Slow down, baby. Slow down. We have all night."

She positioned herself over him as he rolled on a condom. He sat up and slid himself meticulously into her vagina. She moved her body up and down, and wet everything as soon as he entered her.

"Oh.... Oh, give it all to me. Put your big ass on me good."

Pushing herself down firm she began to ride him. She was slow at first and moved faster as he met her in mid air. Alex continued his delight with her titties and squeezed her ass tightly with each stroke.

"Oh, Alex. Alex, baby. I'm what you need. Take it. Take it all like that…harder."

Alex pumped his body up and down furiously. He felt her opening up wider to accept him as he overdosed on a legal high.

His breathing was as hot and hard as he was.

He panted. "I didn't know you could do this to me…yeah…"

His hands lost control as he slapped her ass cheeks in unison. His arms riveted in a cocoa motion that made him repeat the smacks over and over.

"All these titties…all this ass…ahh…"

A special dark contraction controlled him.

"Ahhh, damn, Delv…"

She moved her hips back and forth along with her up and down motion, while holding Alex within her.

He went wild.

"Hold on, baby. Oh…"

As she felt him release, she let him go and began to relax her body on his. He kissed her on the lips and chest before laying back spread eagle on the bed. She then rose up off of him and lay next to him, kissing his face all over as they mellowed with the moment.

The conqueror spoke. "Are you okay? Did you enjoy me?"

"Whew, girl. Yes. Hell yes. I'm a little embarrassed though. I've been with two and three women and have never,

I mean never, ever, uh, well you know. What did you do to me?"

She let out a sexy chuckle and kissed him again before responding.

"I made you feel good that's all. Real good. Just because I'm big doesn't mean I don't know what I'm doing, or how to please a man."

"I see. I honestly didn't know what to expect but I didn't expect that. How did you learn to move like that?"

"Imagination. I imagined you were here and when you finally came, well…"

Alex rolled over on top of her and snuggled his neck into hers.

"Sooooo, may I spend the night with you or do I have to leave?"

"So you like Delvina do you now?"

He pressed his face deeper into her in an attempt to hide his expression. She kissed his cheek as she answered.

"It's okay, baby. I already know the answer. We won't make this a one night stand; let's try for two."

42nd Street

Lately our relationship has been difficult. He says this — I say that, which amounts to no one understanding anything. We've been on a trip with no destination — constant signals and lane changes that cause accidents, which lead to arguments. He is wrong and I'm not right. Love is worth fighting for, but when you fight each other, what will the victor have left to enjoy?

After repeated arguments over a love that seems to hard to obtain, we decided to call a truce. A do-over of sorts.

Time had never been much of a friend to us. Actually, spending time alone just being "us" was a mystery in our relationship. Our truce was to consist of eight hours of time alone in public where we were to behave like new lovers. We wouldn't speak of the ills that plagued our union, nor would we talk about who had broken us, and what we could do to fix our situation.

We made a date to meet on 42nd Street. The lights, the hustle, and most of the positive energy that flowed through the street might help bring us back together. Our lives were spinning chaos that fused lust and hate. Accusing, choosing — fabrications that became believable. It hoped that 42nd Street would make everything corrupt cool.

As I rode the train to meet my ex-fiancé, I thought of the words he'd whispered in my ear the last time we were together. His voice was low and filled with me.

"Make love to your husband."

Over and over again he whispered those words to me. Each time he spoke I took him for a swim. My canal filled and he performed Olympic strokes to handle what I gave him. Sometimes I thought he and I would travel this life-journey together to the end. Maybe today on 42nd Street my doubts will disappear.

We planned to meet outside of B.B. Kings. Neither one of us had ever dined there, so a new atmosphere was the perfect place for a fresh start.

A gentle breeze greeted me as I made my way up the subway stairs. I pulled my lamb coat belt a little tighter thinking it would stop my heart from bounding out of my chest and over to him. His face was the first one that I saw. The street was crowded with people rushing leisurely to go nowhere. He stood tall awaiting someone that he used to love. Things were so bad that I didn't have any idea how he felt about me anymore. I thought I still loved him, but I wasn't really sure.

The traffic seemed to stop as he made his way across the street to me. Although I had been with this man for over three years, I was glued in the moment. The surroundings reminded me that I still held something for him. Today I would find out if I should drop it, or keep holding on until we fused together and became one.

"Hey, baby."

I was still his baby. That was a sign of something.

"Hey."

Our hands joined and locked as we turned together and began walking. I'd walk anywhere, regardless of the distance, if that would keep us together.

"You hungry?"

He cared how I felt. Another sign.

"Actually, I'm more nervous than anything. "

He stopped and pulled me to the side. We stood underneath a theater awning. Another Hollywood classic was in the making.

"Vanajh, I love you. I'm here to prove that. I've done some stupid shit lately, but I love you.

My chest burst and the water came from my eyes. Tears rolled in his sincerity. It covered his face.

"Charles, I know you do. Tell me – what is it that I'm doing wrong? Why can't I seem to please you anymore?"

I had been a singer since I was born. At the age of eight I fell in love with Billie Holliday, Ella Fitzgerald and Diana Ross. My life was created for me to be a jazz singing diva. When Charles and I met my career had begun to blossom. The more it took off, the angrier he became. Charles was included in every decision that I made and he was never satisfied. My love for singing became his hate for me. Everyone told me to let Charles go – that a jealous man would rather lay with another man that see his woman successful. That analogy was too harsh for me to understand. Music and Charles belonged to me and I didn't want to let either one of them go.

His eyes never lied to me. In them I saw a want and a need for a jigsaw puzzle piece that had been missing. A void that grew deeper and deeper that he enabled to never be filled. Hate – anger – jealousy – rage- love didn't seem to fit in his void.

"All I can say is I'm sorry. I want you to have the world. I want you to rule it. I will deal with this. It's just that...well, I've never had a woman like you."

The first time he said that I took it as a compliment. Those words made me feel that I was the first woman in his life that mattered. Never having a woman like me meant that he had never been in love before. I was his first. Hearing those words today makes me ill. He never had a woman like me means that he never wanted to hurt someone so bad.

During our first two years Charles would make sure that I knew he loved me. He'd show up at the studio on the days that I did back-up work with hot tea to soothe my voice. Other times he'd call me just to see how I was doing and ask if I needed anything. Those sweet encounters became ones that held fact-finding properties otherwise known as stalker behavior. Still, I loved him; I wanted him through it all.

We stood facing each other oblivious to the activity around us. A light rain began to fall. My imagination took control. The cameras began filming a love scene that trained actors could never play. The ticket price for us couldn't be paid. It was then that I knew I had to battle for my heart's peace.

"Let's go inside of the theater. I want to make a movie."

Charles smiled, knowing that I still desired him. A relationship requires work – overtime, and a soul that's willing to heal from hurt. All three of my boxes were checked. I was ready.

We entered the theater and all doubts were left lying on 42nd Street. The eight dollar and seventy-five cent matinee fee was a nonchalant gesture to pay for us. Usually, Charles complained about anything he could form words around. Change takes effort. He was willing to change for us.

We paid for a movie that would watch us. After giving our tickets to the door usher, we took the stub and strolled down the hall in love.

We gently stepped into the theater doors like people who were about to misbehave.

"Vanajh, you know we can get arrested for this?"

"Are you scared?"

Charles hesitated before he spoke. The previews were on the screen and the theater was still light. His face softened and his eyes, oh his seductive eyes, answered for him.

"I didn't think you were. I want to sit in the front row on your lap. You ready?"

"Baby this is why I want you. You're daring, but we both have to think about our careers. How about we sit in the back row this time and the next..."

When Charles wasn't flying off the handle about something diminutive he was sensible and smart. This was the man that I wanted. Today I wanted to ride him until he returned and stayed forever.

Charles took my hand and led me to the middle of the last row. The lights dimmed and the movie began to play. There weren't many other people in the theater and if they were, I really didn't notice. There were no people sitting directly in front of us and if they were, umph, they were in for a best picture nominated flick.

Sitting side-by-side we held hands as he leaned into my neck. He left his moist lip prints all over it as he moved up to my ear – "Vanajh, marry me," – and he continued kissing me back down to my neck.

We used to talk about marriage and how it would be. He would cut the grass and wash the cars, and I would cook four dinner meals, five breakfast meals, and prepare our lunch everyday. Sometimes he would be the kitchen aide and I would be the maintenance person. Well laid plains that became sidetracked in anger.

With our faces towards each other our lips pressed deep. I sucked his tongue and tried to swallow it whole. Charles is that thing I want.

Kissing always aroused us. Our lips fit − overlapping, under lapping, and sliding in and out. They just fit. I knew he was ready for me. Each time we looked at one another, we were ready. An inborn passion that kept manifesting throughout.

His tongue roamed my mouth as his hand massaged mine. And then he did what I have wanted him to do without my asking. He slid my fantasy, my dream, the ring that only my future husband could give me on my finger.

Pulling away he said, "Vanajh, marry me."

"Yes."

When Charles was around it didn't take much for me. I had on a skirt with knee-high boots that he simply adored. I slid my coat off and eased myself over onto his lap. He moved my thong over, spread my lips and entered me slow. He held my hips and slid his body down a bit in the chair. I could feel him and wanted to scream.

His voice was low. "Vanajh, you still got the best pussy I ever had."

I could hear him breathing. My head fell forward on the seat in front of me and I bit my wrist. Too big and too hard didn't equal silence. He was playing to win.

His hands slid from my waist down to my inner thighs.

"Oh, no…what are you doing?"

"Shhh. Let me have you."

He pulled my thighs out to the side and my ass back towards him. Slowly he moved me up and down and his body began to tense. I knew he was nervous and excited, and although he wanted me, he wanted to cum quick. As usual, I beat him to it.

"Yeah, baby, yeah, slide that sweet stuff all over me."

The music in the movie went loud and Charles used it to his advantage. He let out a moan while he released. I stayed on his lap after he lowered my legs, somehow thinking that things would change if I moved.

"Hey, are you alright?"

His voice was the same way as in the beginning. Maybe this worked.

"Yeah. I was just thinking."

Charles helped my reposition myself in the seat next to him. Holding hands once again we stared at the screen that had been watching us.

"Vanajh, I promise…no more accusations, no more games. A ring has no end and neither does the way I feel about you."

I looked at the brilliance on my finger and then looked at Charles and smiled. 42nd Street was more than a tourist attraction for us. It brought back the excitement in us, which made us we again.

"Are you sure, baby?"

His lips met mine and I knew. The questions, the doubts, and the insecurities would subside. When we walked out of the darkness and back into the hustle and bright lights, Charles and I would become two restored lovers due to the magic of 42nd Street – a street that I would come to daily in order to keep what we had flourishing.

New Year's Eva

For the past week, all Eva could think about was Marisol. When Sheila arrived for their Christmas gift-wrapping party, neither she nor Marisol mentioned the fact that they almost kissed. Sheila didn't know about the sexually wrapped box or of its contents. When they walked into the den they didn't see the gift. Marisol had placed the items back in the box, and hid it under a magazine rack in the corner of the room. The night went by with the three of them laughing, talking of their plans for the New Year, and Eva and Marisol stealing glances at each other.

Now, as Eva dressed for the New Year's party at the San Diego Pier Yacht Club, she wondered what would it be like to be with a woman. At the age of twenty-nine she had been with her share, and always purchased toys that kept her stimulated on desperate nights. Still, she desired the touch of a mate. Would a woman's touch ease her in all the right places?

What she had in mind for the night, she wasn't sure, but she wore the black teddy that Marisol gave her under her beaded dress. It made her feel sexy that someone wanted to see her in it, and that the someone was a beautiful woman.

Marisol's family owned the club and the three of them decided to end the year with a good old-fashioned New Year's Eve party. No freaky group sex, but instead, sharing the plans of the coming year with people who they were close to. Marisol was the Senior Vice President of Affairs and went all out to make the club look beyond grand. The noisemakers were small boats and water gadgets, the buffet table was filled with foods and delicacies from around the world, and there was champagne flowing from fountains made to look like anchors. She was already there so she sent a limousine to pick up Sheila and Eva. They rode in luxury while sipping champagne and listening to the latest sounds.

"Girl, Marisol knows how to treat a woman doesn't she?"

Eva frowned a bit before she answered.

"I wouldn't know. Do you?"

"Ahh, you're catching feelings aren't you? I hear a bit of jealousy in your voice. What have you and Marisol been up to anyway?"

Squirming from the sudden moistness between her legs she shook her head indicating that she knew nothing of what Sheila mentioned.

"I felt a vibe from the both of you when we were getting the presents together. And you two sure looked chummy at the T-Xtasy. What's up?"

Before Eva could answer the limo stopped and the driver was escorting them out. Marisol stood at the door wearing a tight silver mini dress that pushed her breasts up and her booty out. Sheila watched the expression on Eva's face out of the corner of her eye.

"Uh-huh, somebody is in love."

They all hugged each other when they reached the entrance.

"You ladies look good. How was the ride?"

"The ride was bangin'! Now let me go and find the seafood bar and a man. For the first time I actually want a man and crabs!"

The three of them laughed as Sheila walked towards the buffet area. Marisol's brother met her when she was halfway there, and the two of them would probably be inseparable for the remainder of the night.

Marisol turned her attentions to Eva.

"Eva, you look beautiful. I'm sorry I didn't call you today. I wanted you to have some space and not crowd you."

Running her eyes up and down Marisol's body slowly enticed her. She tried to swallow her feelings, but they revealed themselves anyway.

"I've been thinking about you all week. Marisol, what do you want from me?"

"Follow me."

Marisol took Eva's hand and led her down a long hall away from the festivities. The leather sofa became their timeout zone.

Running her hands through her hair Marisol asked, "Would you like a glass of wine?"

Softly Eva replied, "I just want to talk. What do you want?"

Sliding down from the sofa and perched herself on her knees would make her plea complete. She rested her hands on Eva's thighs.

"I want to be with you. I think you're beautiful. I want to savor in the small of your back while I smell the enchanted scent of you. I can take care of you. Whatever you need I will provide."

Marisol lifted her hand and kissed it lightly.

"Eva, we can do this. No, I'm not the prince you've been waiting for to save you, but the princess who wants to give you what you need. Let me give it all to you."

Marisol kissed her hand again. Eva pulled her back up and they both stood. Their eyes locked, and within them they saw what they were missing. Their lips met. Sexy, slow, and seductive, they touched. Marisol lowered her hands and felt Eva's ass. It was firm and soft. It was hers.

They continued to kiss. Eva moved her lips around Marisol's face and down her neck. She continued further and slid them over her cleavage.

"Ay, Mami, ooh…"

A heated explosion joined them together. "Wait, Eva, I don't want you here like this. I want to make it extraordinary for you. After the party, will you come home with me? Can I be your first and only lover in the New Year?"

"Yes, Mami, yes…"

That night they danced themselves into a love that could be nurtured and grow. The previous parties they attended were special, but this one was deluxe. At midnight balloons dropped, horns blew, and toasts were made.

"Happy New Year, Mami…"

A secret love came to light as their tongues erotically tussled. As Marisol kissed her new love, she vowed to make this the best New Year's Eva would ever have.

Dear Diary

June 18, 2008

It's been a year and nothing has changed. He still controls my mind. When I awoke this morning with nothing to do, my life functioned in a slow erotic motion. My first release of the day came as I did my ritual of using the bathroom. From staring in the mirror, to the shower and then the water, soap and lather, I pretended that he was watching me. To up my sexual ante I added the imagined tidbit of he and her having an argument. She knew where he had stayed the night, and at the particular time of my shower, she cried that her dark lover was with me.

I washed and dried in detailed motion. The towel circled my nipples until they hardened. Slowly I slid the towel around my body, concentrating on my navel and the birth line that led to his pleasure. He smiled thinking of what would soon be his.

Before I stepped out of the bathroom, I slid my feet into the black six-inch stiletto pumps that stood waiting for me. His eyes followed my naked body down the hallway and back into the bedroom. The heels lifted my ass and made my long legs seem eternal. My body would be the temple that never ended for him.

In my bedroom, I lit candles. He stood at the doorway watching me while she lay in her bed crying. The sensuous smell of mango, mocha and me filled the room. I pulled the covers back to reveal the place where we would lay together. My arms reached out to welcome him and my heart opened up to release my luv to him. For some reason he didn't move.

The same year that it has been for me, it has been for him. His feelings haven't changed. He still luvs her. The tears I wished on her stayed with me. Why does she continue to do "it" for him? Why do I continue to wonder why?

Uhmmm…I still want her man. The way I would suck his body, things that protruded, things that I had to find, uhmmm, I'd miss nothing. Here I stand wet with wonder and naked with longing. The scene is set but a key piece is missing. Shall I continue to wait for him to luvme?

LuvMe is the second of numerous works that will come from Wanda D. Hudson. Her first novel, Wait for Love: A Black Girl's Story, is available at all major booksellers.

Miss Hudson has a story included in the NY Times Bestseller Zane anthology, Succulent - Chocolate Flava ll, which is available now.

Check out Purple Panties, Miss Hudson is in that Zane anthology as well.

Please visit Wanda D. Hudson's website – www.wandadhudson.com - to read excerpts and to stay in the know about this sexy dynamic writer.

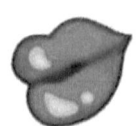

Miss Luv's Books